THE ACCIDENT

Kate Hendrick was born in 1983. She is a teacher of visual arts and photography, and lives in Sydney with her husband and daughter.

THE
ACCIDENT

KATE HENDRICK

TEXT PUBLISHING MELBOURNE AUSTRALIA

textpublishing.com.au

The Text Publishing Company
Swann House
22 William Street
Melbourne Victoria 3000
Australia

First published by The Text Publishing Company 2013

Design by Imogen Stubbs
Typeset by J&M Typesetting

Printed and bound in Australia by Griffin Press, an Accredited ISO AS/NZS 14001:2004 Environmental Management System printer

National Library of Australia Cataloguing-in-Publication entry
Author: Hendrick, Kate, author.
Title: The accident / by Kate Hendrick.
ISBN: 9781921922855 (paperback)
ISBN: 9781921921544 (ebook)
Dewey Number: A823.4

For my family,
who have long tolerated my creative endeavours.

No man is an island

JOHN DONNE

Phones ringing, the constant chug of the photocopiers, the whirr of the fans. People talking, walking, typing… After the months at home I'd forgotten how busy the world can be.

I'm sweating. Something else I'd forgotten about schools—no air conditioning. It's thirty-nine degrees today and I'm sticking to the plastic chair. I know when I get up I'll leave a sweat patch and there's not much I can do about it.

My mind throws up a mental image of the pool, sparkling blue in the brilliant mid-morning light. If only…

'Sarah?' The principal.

I have never dealt with a woman principal before.

She's tall, and didn't smile once during the interview. I get uncomfortable around people who don't smile.

There is a girl beside her. Tall, perfectly straight honey-blonde hair, socks pulled up. Apparently that's the fashion now. It's hard to keep up. She has a prefect badge pinned to her collar. No jewellery: school rules. The only evidence I can see that she and I exist in the same climatic region is a thin sheen of sweat under her hairline. Other than that, she looks as perfect as a Barbie doll.

'This is Sarah Bancroft. She'll show you around and answer any questions you might have.'

Sarah and Sarah. I wonder if somebody thought that was cutesy or if it's just a coincidence. I nod and stand. Discreetly unstick my skirt from the back of my legs. Sarah Bancroft offers me a cool half smile and gestures. 'Let's go.'

I get the impression this is not the first time she's had to play tour guide. Two strides ahead, she leads me down corridors and through identical donut-shaped blocks, throwing out brief descriptions. Toilets, English staff room, computer rooms, library, science, maths…

We pass a group of senior students sitting at cafe-style tables. A few of them are wearing year twelve jerseys with the year in giant numbers on the back. I think of the jersey buried somewhere in the bottom of my wardrobe with last year's date on the back and I wonder what I'm doing here.

Sarah Bancroft's still talking. 'You're in my art class. We've got Shepherd. Her room is the one at the end.' She pauses, glances at the timetable in her hands. 'You've got drama now. It's the room downstairs with the blacked-out windows. Any questions?'

It's a long room, with black-painted walls and heavy drapes on runners around one end. Students are lounging around on the carpeted floor when I enter, deep in trivial conversations. The voices pause for no more than a second as they look up. I'm a stranger, a new specimen, but only worth a quick glance. I'm neither a threat nor particularly interesting.

That seems to be how it goes throughout the day. The cliques are fully formed, the social hierarchies calcified. Part of me feels like I'm back at St Ives. Pulling on my school shoes brought it back the strongest. There was a drip of turquoise paint on one, the colour of oxidised copper like Michelangelo's outdoor David, a moment that made me catch my breath and hold it; and as long as I didn't let go I could stay there in my old classroom, my old school. Old life.

It's a parallel universe. The school is unfamiliar, the uniform a different colour, but it's ultimately all the same. Kids swarming over the quadrangle and through the corridors between classes. Kicking balls, shouting, wrestling, swearing. The smell of sweat and too much deodorant and spearmint gum. I feel camouflaged at first, but as the day goes on I'm yearning for my bedroom.

Maths, English, history, and then I have art last. The smells hit me as I enter: turps, clay, photographic chemicals, fresh lino shavings and paint.

My art teacher is reassuringly scatty. She has frizzy brown hair with an inch of grey at the roots and wears her school keys on a chain, spaced out like charms on a giant jangling necklace. She tugs at it, trying to find the right key for the storeroom. The fans click in a drowsy rhythm. Sarah Bancroft and her friends lounge near the window drinking bottled water and talking about boys.

It's fifty-two minutes of lazy disorder. Nobody has brought their art diary. My name hasn't been added to the roll. I spell it for her.

'Starke. With an e.'

I hit the water with my clothes on. Just dive straight in, shoes and all. Mum will go mental but I don't care. It's cold and fresh and blue and everything I want it to be. I skim along the bottom of the pool till I reach the end, then I tumble and push off, stroking underwater till I get back to the shallow end and come up gasping.

I leave a trail through the house, a long line of drips punctuated by wet clothes. Shoes, green checked skirt, white blouse, socks. I know I'll get used to them but I haven't yet; they still feel foreign. Forest green, like Christmas trees.

Mum's locked Iago in the laundry. It's been months

since he's been locked away and I can hear him scratching and barking as he hears me getting closer. I open the laundry door and he almost bowls me over. I manage to push him down but not before I get half a dozen angry red scratches on my bare stomach. 'Yago...' It's only half-hearted scolding, though. He's already on his back, seeming to grin at the sound of his nickname and madly waving his tail, ready for a tummy rub.

'You're such a baby.' I scratch him with my bare foot and dump the bundle of wet clothes into the laundry tub. I make half an effort to wring them out, then chuck them in the washing machine and put them on to spin. I give up trying to squeeze the water out of my school shoes and put them on the outdoor table to dry and harden in the afternoon sun.

More wet footprints and the scraping and scrambling of dog claws on tiles as we head into the kitchen. There's a Post-it on the fridge from Mum asking me to marinate a steak.

It's just past four. Already my new school feels a world away. I wander round the house in my wet underwear, knowing I have at least two hours till Mum or Alan comes home. What now? I sit on the floor in my room staring at the stack of canvases I got for my birthday, avoiding the decision. Eventually I go and marinate the steak because I know if I forget Mum will act as if I've burnt the house down. Iago is at my feet whining as I slice open the meat tray. I peel a corner off one piece and hold it out to him; he licks my hand clean then looks up at me, expectant.

'Sorry buddy, that's all you get for now.'

I cook the way I think Mum would cook if she ever actually tried. I vaguely know the recipe Alan uses—vegetable oil, soy sauce, Worcestershire, red wine vinegar, lemon juice, onions and garlic—but I don't worry too much about the quantities. I toss in some Dijon mustard and grind some pepper over the top, then sniff the mix. Seems okay; I lower the steak into the bowl and prod at it until it's immersed. Starke cuisine.

Iago's at my feet, still whining. I put the empty meat tray down on the floor for him to lick as I pack away the ingredients. He nudges it around as he licks it and I have to fish it out from under the fridge.

Later we sit on the couch and I scratch his belly and try to absorb some of his satisfaction with life.

Dinner is never silent but often, lately, it's only Mum who does the talking. She's working on a terrace house in Paddington, and the owners want a different theme for every room.

'Africa in the lounge room, India in the dining room—they've got boxes full of fabric and artifacts. Saris as curtains, *aiuto*!' She throws her hands up in the air when she slips into Italian. '*Terribile!* And the wife won't listen to a word I say. Just pig-headed.'

Diplomatic relations have never been Mum's thing.

She has that typical artist's approach to everything—egocentric—which means constant conflict between what her clients want and what she intends to do for them. She usually talks them around to doing it her way, and ninety-nine percent of the time they end up thanking her for it. And I have to admit, she does impressive work. She's just not a team player.

There's ten more minutes detailing a new chrome and leather sofa before she remembers to ask, 'How was your first day?'

I shrug. How does she expect me to put it into words? 'All right.'

I find Alan stacking the dishwasher. I don't think he said a single word during dinner. Mum doesn't notice.

I like Alan. I always have. He has infinite patience with Mum. I've never really understood how they ended up with each other, because they're complete opposites in every way, but I'm thankful that they did. He's the rational one when Mum's off the planet, which is most of the time. He's calm. I literally can't remember ever hearing him raise his voice.

'So what was it like to be back?'

I think about it. 'A bit weird. You know, it's a new school, but in the end it's all just kinda the same...'

In the past there would have been some sort of crack about if there were any good-looking boys, some sort of tease, but he just nods. Not only because it's somehow a serious thing, but because we've all become more sober about everything. He and Mum used to laugh like crazy, all the time.

'Do you think there's a point where it gets back to normal?' I ask suddenly.

He's not surprised. He knows exactly what I'm talking about. 'I think we end up with a new kind of normal,' he answers slowly.

'But there's got to be a point where we can start to… you know.'

'Move on?'

'Yeah.'

He thinks longer this time. 'I've seen a lot of people try to move on from different things. Some people manage it, others don't. Sometimes they can't because they still need answers. They still have questions.'

Do we? I can only think of one.

'Like: "Why did it happen"?'

He nods. 'That's usually the big one.'

'What do you tell people when they ask that?'

'I tell them that we can't always control what happens to us. But we can control how we respond to it.' He shrugs. 'After twenty years that's still the best I've got.'

Iago is snoring, his fat barrel body stretched out on my rug. The rest of the house is dark and silent and sleeping. It's almost twelve and I'm wasting time on YouTube because I don't want to sleep or can't or something.

It's a clear night, more stars than usual, twinkling away. Robbie had a telescope and he used to explain the different constellations to me, but I could never see them and he'd run out of patience.

I turn to shut down my computer and the pile of canvases in the corner catches my eye.

'I don't know what to do.' I say it out loud. I gaze around the room, staring for a long moment at my photo wall, feeling the familiar stir of indecision, of feeling like I should be doing something but I don't know what.

Right in the middle of my photo wall is a text collage I spent hours making from newspaper headlines.

You must be the change you wish to see in the world.

Gandhi said that; it used to fire me up, and now it only makes me feel tired. It's just not so simple anymore.

I think about Alan's words. We can't control the things that happen to us; we can only control how we respond to them. Maybe that thought placates some people, but Mum would have killed him if he'd tried to use that on her.

Still…I wonder if she ever asks him that question. I wonder what he says. I wonder what they think when they remember that night, and what it cost us all.

It's a dream I've had a hundred times. I know it so well my subconscious is just along for the ride, a director standing in the wings mouthing the lines while the actors take over on stage.

She comes home with a shiny clunky metal thing. When I ask she says, 'It's a shredder, Will. For turning paper into snow.' Then she starts to pull all her old bundles of manuscripts down from the top of the wardrobe, where Dad once kept his things. She rips the brown paper off one and feeds the cover sheet through. We watch with goosebumps as the machine churns and the paper is sliced into long, white strips.

'I want to try! My turn!' we all yell, and Mum stands aside to let us slice open the bundles and feed the pages

through, never once pausing to look at the closely typed words covering them. Morgan is sent off for buckets to catch the strips, and when we finish the last pages Mum stands at the top of the stairs and tips the bucketfuls down over us. One at a time, watching the pieces float down like snow, while we dance underneath like the heathens our grandmother says we are.

Two thumps and then a clatter like somebody has upended a bin full of tin cans. My eyes snap open to a dark bedroom. It was afternoon before.

I flip on the light. *Life of Pi* is still open beside me, face down on the rumpled covers. Disoriented, I slide the bookmark in and push myself up off the bed, listening to Morgan banging and swearing in the kitchen.

It only takes Morgan thirty seconds to make a mess. Her school bag and folder are dumped in the middle of the rug, papers falling out everywhere. On the kitchen counter is a torn paper bag. Spray cans have tumbled out, rolled onto the floor and scattered around the room. In her arms she holds a huge, awkward roll of canvas.

'What's that?'

'Backdrop.'

There's a scowl on her face as usual. She's in a foul mood. She's been in it for at least the last year and a half. I remember when she was little I'd give her piggyback rides, and she thought I was the world's best big brother. Now I reckon she's got a better chance of carrying me.

11

She drags the canvas outside, comes back for the spray paint. I follow her, watching from the doorway as she spreads the canvas over the grass, selects a can and starts going over the image. The paint comes in hisses and spurts.

There's a rumble of thunder in the distance. I saw clouds drifting in earlier, but figured they'd be gone by now. It hasn't rained in forever. For months all they've talked about on the news and weather reports is drought and water restrictions. Now the night sky is filled with serious-looking storm clouds.

I see Morgan glance upwards, gauging whether it'll rain in the next few minutes…Nah; worth the risk. She wipes her painty fingertips on the old pyjama top she's thrown on and holds the spray can blindly out to me as she rummages through the cans and lids on the ground. 'Can you shake this for me? It's running out.'

I stand obediently shaking the can, considering the backdrop stretched under the floodlight. At least three metres wide by two high. It looks almost finished, a dark stormy sky and wild trees with branches clawing out in every direction. They're doing *King Lear*. Morgan's playing Cordelia, though I only found that out through other people. Morgan doesn't really tell me things. I guess most sisters don't tell their brothers stuff.

'Looks good.'

A grunt; she's working. I take the hint and leave her to it.

After dinner she flops on the couch to watch TV, her usual slack self. The sky is rumbling; every once in a while there's a particularly forceful roll of thunder and the TV screen flickers. Then one crashing strike, and the lights go out as the rain starts to pound down outside.

'Shit.' Morgan jumps up off the couch, sending cushions flying. 'The backdrop.'

So long, drought. The backyard is a quagmire. The storm is in full swing: rain bucketing down, lightning bolts bouncing around the sky. I stand just inside the door, hovering as Morgan dashes out. She's soaked within seconds, her socks wet and flopping as she sloshes through the grass, trying to drag the canvas under the eaves. I almost call out and tell her not to bother now, it's too late, but I don't. I watch as she struggles with it, as the wind catches it. It's heavy with all the absorbed water, far too big for one person to wrangle. She probably has bigger muscles than I do, but still. She drags from one corner, then another. It's mostly off the grass but the rain, driven by the wind, still pelts down on it under the eaves. Lost cause. Give it up, Morgan.

She does eventually, and pushes back past me inside, dripping wet.

'Thanks for helping.'

'I didn't think it was worth...' She's not interested.

She heads towards the bathroom, leaving a trail of muddy sock prints on the hardwood.

I can't sleep. Even after Morgan has mumbled a good-night and disappeared into her room, I roam around the house, too restless to stop and settle down. Occasionally I can hear Mum moving around upstairs but she doesn't come down to check on us. It'd take more than a storm and blackout to get her out of her room.

The storm passes, leaving an eerie stillness outside, and when I stand at the lounge room windows and look out I can see the front yard is a mess of fallen branches and leaves. The entire street is dark. In a few windows I can see the flickers of candlelight or roving torches, otherwise it's just slivers of moonlight as the clouds start to clear.

It's silent upstairs and I wonder what Mum is doing, whether her laptop battery has enough charge to last her. It's nearly midnight, but she never gets to bed before about two. Morgan will be buried under the doona, her iPod lulling her to sleep.

I try to do some study by torchlight, but it's more effort than it's worth trying to hold the torch at the right angle. Finally I give up and put on my running shoes.

It's only mid-May but it's cold outside. I can see my breath as I do a few quick stretches before taking off down the street. The moonlight paints everything silver, and the fallen branches shiny with raindrops smell of fresh eucalyptus and pine. I know by daylight the storm damage will seem far more devastating than it does now.

My feet fall easily into rhythm. I run on the road, erratic as I circle the wide puddles of overflowing storm-water drains. I turn onto Sentinel Avenue and up ahead there are the lights and trucks and commotion of the State Emergency Service, tying a massive tarp over somebody's damaged roof. A red gum split by lightning has crashed through their lounge room window.

'Hail the size of golf balls up north,' I overhear one of the SES workers calling to another across the rooftop. Maybe, I think to myself, I should join the SES. Learn how to climb on roofs and use chainsaws instead of being stuck in my room with a book like a girl. Yeah; I'd last a week.

I push onwards, trying to pick up my pace. At the end of Sentinel there's two choices—swing right for home or left to do the bigger loop alongside Galbraith Gorge. It's late and it's dark and my chest is burning but I know if I head home now I won't be tired enough to sleep. I take a left, loving the meaty slap of my sneakers on the wet road. The round trip's only three k or so, but it takes me nearly half an hour in the dark. The street-lights are still out and in some places the trees are so thick the moonlight barely reaches through.

Our street is dark and quiet. Obviously we missed the worst of the storm, because it seems everybody here has long gone to bed. I slow to a walk as I approach our house. Hands behind my head, deep breaths; realising there's at least one other person still awake. I can hear Kayla next door, practising quietly. She normally plays her real drums in the afternoons when most neighbours are still at work, but sometimes when I'm awake late at night I can hear the low thud of her practice pads through my open window. It's a bit creepy sometimes, like a tribal beat forming the background for human sacrifice. She's weird enough, I wouldn't put it past her.

A red Echo is parked on an angle under the Moreton Bay fig, bonnet clean and shiny after the rain. My stomach tightens.

Lauren.

The front entryway is dark and empty. I slip inside and I've just about made it to my bedroom when I see yellow light and steam spilling out from under the bathroom door. I'm still staring and the door suddenly opens.

Skeletal.

It's the first word that comes into my mind. The harsh shadow created by the torchlight probably doesn't help. She's cut her hair short, and it's sticking out all over the place, wet. There are hollows under her eyes and her skin is stretched tightly across her cheekbones. Her arms are muscled—like Morgan's more than mine—but they look stringy and her black singlet and dark striped pyjama pants hang off her. I look at her and I know she doesn't look normal.

For a long second she just stares at me. She wasn't expecting to have to face somebody so soon. Then, without a sound, she squeezes past. I listen to her retreating footsteps and the gentle click as she pulls her door shut.

Morgan doesn't confide in me, but I think that I do at least exist in her little self-centred world, somewhere on the periphery. It'd be optimistic to think she still sees me as her big brother, but maybe there's a tiny part of her brain that knows we're family and we have to be there for each other.

But to Lauren…At best, she chooses her words to cut me down. At worst, she treats me like I don't exist at all.

Thursday. Terry is at the kitchen bench sorting the mail when I get in. Only half an hour till dinner but damn I'm starving. Grab the Froot Loops from the cupboard. Perch on a bar stool, eating dry handfuls.

Terry's tall with a shaved head. I saw photos of him once before he shaved it, gawky and thinning on top. Made him look a lot older. Shaved, it gives him a bit of attitude. He's got a sense of humour when he gets a chance to let it off the leash. We get along all right.

'Hey, Eliat. How was school?'

'Punch-ups, obscenities, drug bust…Just the usual.'

'And who said no to a private school?'

'You kidding? You couldn't write anything that good.'

Smiles. Pours himself juice.

'You still all right for Saturday night?'

'Yeah. Party's all organised. Got the pot stashed under my mattress and the bedrooms set up for underage sexual encounters.'

He's used to me. He snorts like he gets the irony. 'You know if Rose-Marie ever hears you talking like that, she'll never leave you alone again.'

'Terry, I'm your A-grade student, remember? Besides, what's the point of a fake ID if you never go out?'

'With Tash in tow, I suppose?'

'Nah, she'll be right. She loves it here on her own. Put The Wiggles on and crank up the volume.'

Shakes his head, pretends to be horrified. 'Seriously, if Rose-Marie heard you…'

'All right, relax. Tash'll be in bed by seven and I'll be churning out two thousand words on *Othello*. Might be on a bit of a caffeine high by the time you get home, and I can't guarantee not to get into your chocolate stash if things get serious. Better?'

'Much.' Pulls out the wok. 'How was the driving lesson?'

'Too many one-way streets in the city, too many traffic lights. I stalled again. Haven't done that in weeks. But I guess the upside is I didn't run into anyone…'

'Progress.'

'That you, Eliat?' Rose-Marie calling from upstairs. Time to get Tash out of the bath.

'Gotta go.' I put the box of Froot Loops down on the bench and climb off the bar stool.

I'm at the bottom of the stairs when Terry calls after me. 'One last thing…' He looks serious but I know his style.

'Hands off your chocolate?'

'If you want to see your eighteenth birthday.'

It's warm in the bathroom. The heat and smell of a recent load through the dryer. Tash is singing to herself as she wriggles and slides around in the tub, her shiny wet bottom breaking the surface. Rose-Marie is folding socks with the same cheerful patience she brings to any task, no matter how unpleasant or mundane. Rose-Marie irritates me. Not sure why. She's like a sweet fragrance, okay in small doses but overpowering when you get too much. Don't know how Terry ended up with her, really. Sometimes I want to rile her up just to get a break from the sugar.

'How was school?'

When Terry asked it was an opening to joke around. She wants a proper answer and it just seems like too much effort. 'All right.'

She drops the bundle into the basket of clean laundry and lifts it onto her hip. 'She's ready to get out.'

I watch Rose-Marie go, then reach for Tash's towel. 'All right, you heard that. Time's up.'

'Two more!' she pleads.

'Nope, now. Terry's got dinner on.' She loves Terry's cooking.

I get an incomprehensible earful about her day as I lift her out of the tub, dry her off and awkwardly sticky-tab a nappy. She pushes me away when I start dressing her. 'I can do.'

'Yeah, well last time you put your pants on backwards.' Tug her back towards me till we're face to face. Her eyes are big.

'Tomorrow Sat'day?'

'Tomorrow's Friday. It goes Thursday, Friday, then Saturday.'

'When we go zoo?'

'Saturday. Not tomorrow, day after.'

A visit to the zoo is a second birthday present from Terry and Rose-Marie. She hasn't shut up about it since we explained it to her. I don't think she really gets the days of the week but she knows Saturday is when we're going to the zoo.

Dinner is the usual. Tash eats earlier, so it's just the three of us at the table, my least favourite time of the day. I swear Rose-Marie thinks her main purpose in life is to teach me table manners. She's a total Nazi about using the right fork, the right serving implement. It's a relief when she lays off me and turns to Terry.

'Any rain in sight?'

Terry works for the Bureau of Meteorology. This is

Rose-Marie's way of showing interest in his job, and she's asked the frigging question every day since it last rained, which was in fact the twelfth of February. Thanks to Terry, my head is now filled with useless shit like that.

'Nothing yet.' Terry at least manages to vary his answer, and—more impressively—makes it sound like he's actually glad she asked. If I were him I would have told her months ago to just turn on the damn weather channel and look for herself.

The most common cause of drought in Australia is the climate phenomenon called the Southern Oscillation, a major air pressure shift between the Asian and east Pacific regions. Its best-known extreme is El Niño. As I said, useless shit.

Rose-Marie turns back to me. 'We need to talk about schools for Tash.'

'Preschool?'

'No, primary. The good ones fill up early, three or four years ahead. There's a few options around here that we can hopefully still get into. I thought we could sit down and look over some information after dinner.'

Tightening in my stomach. 'Yeah, but can we do it tomorrow? I've got a stack of maths homework.'

She holds my gaze for a long moment, then nods. 'Of course.'

Tash conks out in front of the TV and Rose-Marie puts her to bed. I sit down to do my maths homework but my concentration's shot, thanks to Rose-Marie. I've got enough things going round in my head. I don't need more. I sure as hell don't need to be thinking about something that's three whole years away.

I grab a can of Coke from my bar fridge. Takes me a while to remember where I stashed the Bacardi, but I find it in the bottom of the wardrobe. Top up the can and then re-hide the bottle at the bottom of my Balderdash box.

'You know, hiding booze is a key sign of alcoholism,' Izzy the sage told me once.

'Shut up,' was my answer. 'It's just so Rose-Marie doesn't find it.'

A drink settles my mind enough for me to get through one textbook exercise and start on another. I'm trying to remember how to do rectangular hyperbola when I get interrupted.

'Tash, what are you doing up?'

'I woke up.'

'Well, go back to sleep.'

'I dinna get story.' Rose-Marie got so excited when Tash started talking. Didn't realise from then on she'd never shut up.

'I have to do my homework.'

She comes closer, climbs up onto my lap and nudges my hand aside to see what I'm doing. She's always this way, as if she can't wait to be reading and writing and doing overcomplicated and unnecessary maths problems too.

'What's that?' Absolute favourite question.

'Finding the loci of points in rectangular hyperbola.'

The eyes go past my work, to the can of Coke. The hands reach out for it. I whisk it out of her reach. 'No, mine. You already brushed your teeth.'

I'll get a tantrum now; natural follow-up to not getting what she wants. She'll dig in stubbornly and keep going till she gets it. Well, tough luck, kid. I've been playing this game a lot longer than you have.

Before she can unleash, I tighten my grip around her waist. Take her into her room. It's dark. Rose-Marie forgot to turn on the nightlight. Climb onto her bed— it was another birthday present, graduating from the cot—and grab a random book from the shelf. 'One book, okay? Then I have to go finish my homework.'

Wriggly, impatient, not happy with that book. Elbow in the chest as she climbs over me to choose a different one. *Diary of a Wombat.* 'This one.'

'Okay, this one.' She's had it read to her probably hundreds of times, and like always she wants to race through, tries to turn the pages before I'm done reading them. I read through it once, then she wants it again, then I tuck her in properly, as she tries to wriggle free.

'No, stay there. Rose-Marie'll get mad if you don't go to sleep.'

I leave her there with her room lit blue by the night-light. My maths books lie open, waiting for me, but my concentration is really screwed now. I shut the books and top up the Coke. Stretch out on my bed.

The roof slopes downwards over my bed: it's a real attic bedroom. The ceiling's completely covered in A3 pages I printed off in the school library and taped up there. Took me nearly a week to put together. Izzy came over and stared at it for a full minute or two before she asked me what it was.

'It's a brain, you idiot.'

She couldn't understand why I'd paper my roof with a scientific diagram. Her bedroom walls are an inch thick with years' worth of hot pin-up boys, the less clothes the better far as she's concerned. I didn't bother explaining, she wouldn't understand. She never does.

So this is my bedtime routine. I lie there with my drink and gaze up, tracing the different sections, rolling the names over my tongue. I imagine diving inside, watching the neural connections flash by on all sides, the cerebrum walls stacked with folders and files like on a hard drive, each packed full of data: snapshots, glimpses of memory. The fresh arrivals from today are: the foul odour of a stink bomb in our English classroom, the familiar shudder of the car just before it stalled, the sight of Tash's bare little bottom in the bathtub and the sound of her nonsense singing echoing off the tiles. I sort each incident. I let my mind dwell on the good ones and commit them to memory. Will the rest away. Then I take my mind back, systematic as always.

My first crush, on Matty Jardin in year two.

Being bitten by a dog in kindy.

Fourth birthday, somebody made me a castle cake.

I explore each memory carefully, trying to squeeze out as much detail as possible before moving on. Sometimes, rarely, I get something new, something long filed away. A voice, a glimpse of a face or hands. Impossible to date. Impossible to know if it's even real, or if my mind has simply started manufacturing memories. Making up answers because I don't have them. One hundred billion neurones. Talk about a needle in the haystack.

I scull the rest of the rum and Coke. Make another. The warmth creeps in slowly, lifts me. Rose-Marie can do what she wants. Let her make her plans, I don't care anymore.

Terry and his chocolate.

Rose-Marie and her stupid plans.

Tash.

The darkroom is supposed to be empty, and it's not. The safe lights are on, and I give my eyes a few seconds to adjust and pick out the form at the wet bench. A girl. Maybe my grade, probably a year or two younger. She lifts her paper carefully out of the stop and lowers it into the fixer, then gently rocks the tray so the chemical covers the print. Only once that's done does she look up and notice me.

'Hi.'

I feel foolish, like an intruder. I still feel like an outsider, no matter how many names I learn or how many routines I now find myself flowing through, and it's tiring. I was hoping this would be a sanctuary.

'I'm Sarah. I'm in year twelve. I'm new...'

'Morgan. Year eleven.' She moves a second print out of the wash and shakes the water off it, holding it up to look at it.

'Do you do this in art or as an elective? Photography, I mean.'

'I've got a free period now so Miss Shepherd lets me come here to work. I do the two-unit elective. They don't do it with art classes—too many idiots.' She throws me a grin, and I feel a surge of gratitude. I need a friend.

She puts her print in the drying rack and then moves the other one out of the fixer. 'Are you doing photography for your major work?'

'Maybe. Still deciding.'

'My brother just finished year twelve. He didn't do art, though. He was into the boring subjects—legal studies, that sort of thing.' She pauses. 'Are you going to do some photos?'

'Yeah.' I don't know where everything is kept, though. 'I'm new, so...'

As a tour guide, she's nothing like Sarah Bancroft. She shows me the fridge where the paper is stored, the cupboards where the mixed chemicals go, the squeegee for cleaning down the wet bench. She gives me a running commentary as she goes.

'Processing tanks and black bags are in the storeroom. You have to peg the bags shut at the bottom because they're all torn up. I usually bring it in here just to make sure no light gets in. And lock the door when you come in, if you're by yourself. You're not supposed to because of the chemicals—you know, in case you pass out from fumes or whatever—but if you don't, there's a bunch of guys who'll come in and switch on the white lights. They think it's funny.'

I've brought in a sleeve of negatives from last year. I fish it out of my bag, pick a photo randomly and play around with the enlarger settings. It's been almost a year since I've been in a darkroom, and I need to get my technique back before I can do anything else.

Morgan chats as we work. Even though all I've wanted all morning is to be by myself and have peace and quiet like I'm used to, I don't mind it at all. It reminds me of how Robbie and I used to talk, and it didn't matter whether we were talking about McDonald's or about God and the meaning of life, it just came easily. Even with the extractor churning and Morgan's voice, it feels peaceful.

I drop my first print into the developer, and Morgan leans over to watch as the image emerges.

'That's awesome. Where is that, Europe somewhere?'

'Rome.' It's a narrow side street Robbie and I wandered into while Mum and Alan went for coffee. I loved the uneven cobbled road and the peonies in the window-boxes. There's an old-fashioned bicycle leaning against a wall, and a bunch of motor bikes and scooters outside a gelateria.

'Did you go over on exchange?'

'Family holiday. My mum's Italian. We go over every couple of years to visit all her relatives. She was born here, but you wouldn't know it. She still talks in Italian half the time.'

'You got brothers or sisters or anything?'

It's such a casual, normal question, but my stomach drops, and suddenly I just don't want to be here anymore. I suck in a breath to try to fight down the panic. Force my hands to stay steady as I lift my print out of the developer and drop it into the stop bath. 'No. Just me.'

I'm not prepared for the blinding sunlight. It's a shock after the darkroom. I have to put a hand up to shield my face and wait for my eyes to adjust. The bell has just gone for the end of recess and there's movement everywhere, pushing and shoving and noise. Too much.

I'm supposed to have English now. I feel the anxiety rise back up at the thought of group discussions. Part of me can see it's interesting, the intricacies of plot and theme. The rest of me can't think of anything more pointless than discussing Othello's evolving frame of mind. Part of me realises that, ultimately, stuff like that doesn't actually matter.

Almost before I've made a conscious decision I've started to push my way through the traffic. I duck around the corner of the library then head past the hall. I've never, ever jigged school before, but somehow the thought of getting into trouble for it doesn't bother me.

I'm not even worried that I might get caught. I just know I can't sit through English right now.

It takes me almost an hour to walk home. It's stinking hot and I'm sweating, and my folder and bag are weighed down with books and textbooks, and my leg is really hurting, but I don't care. I feel free again. I feel like I could easily just not go back. Maybe I won't.

The house is cool and quiet, but too empty. I change out of my uniform and take Iago and we head down into the bush, tramping along the overgrown path, trying to keep in the tree-shade. Even so, by the time we get to the creek I have sweat again in every crevice and Iago is panting, his whole body wobbling with the effort. I climb up onto my favourite fallen red gum and sit straddling it over the water, watching the insects zip across the water's surface, darting and diving, while Iago snuffles in the undergrowth. My leg is aching from too much walking and I stretch it out along the log, trying not to think about it, about anything. The sweat on my skin starts to cool and my legs itch from the long grass, but I feel better than I have anywhere else. I close my eyes, listening to the birdsongs and cicadas and Iago as he scavenges.

And I think about that stormy night, about the man. The one the doctors said saved my life. I wonder what he's doing now, and if I'll see him again.

'Would he think that was weird, Yago?'

He looks up at me, ears pricked. I smile. 'What do you reckon? Or will he just think I'm a kid with a crush?'

I don't remember much, but I remember the way he talked to me. It hurt so much that I felt like I was drowning, and his words were the only thing I had to hang onto, the only thing that kept me from giving up and letting myself be swallowed up by the pain, giving up and going with Robbie. I remember his eyes and feeling like I could trust him, that I could literally put my life in his hands, and that he would keep me safe.

I get home and Alan meets me at the door. 'I'm going to pick up dinner. You want to drive?'

He asks me that every time he goes on an errand, as if my previous flat-out refusals haven't been clear enough. I shake my head. 'I'm fine. I've got homework to do.'

He won't give up that easily. 'You can't avoid it forever, you know.'

'You wanna bet?'

He's already tried all the arguments on me, the get-back-on-the-horse encouragement. It doesn't work. Even with the way my leg is, I'd rather walk and catch public transport. Being in a car still scares me, even if I'm with Mum or Alan. I still catch myself sometimes, in the passenger seat, feeling the panic start to rise up as we approach an intersection, and I look down and realise I'm holding on so tight my fingers are white.

I used to be spontaneous. Careless, Mum would say. Now I stress over most decisions, worrying, weighing up the possibilities; what could happen. Getting back behind the wheel of a car is one of the few things I don't need to think about. Some day in the future, maybe. But for now I'm sticking to my guns, and it makes it easy somehow, having at least that one absolute.

before
after
later

I heard a story once, a long time ago. There are some stories that stick with you, they haunt you in one way or another, and this one has. It was about a horse race. One particular jockey wanted badly to win and pushed his horse extra hard. The horse responded, giving the jockey everything it had—its whole body straining forwards, blood pumping madly. And as the little horse propelled itself over the finish line—first place—its heart literally exploded in its chest. It gave everything to win that race and the glory that came with it. It gave up its life so its name would live forever.

My mother is a writer. She has been for as long as I remember. She used to write at all hours of the night. I'd wake up at midnight, two, three a.m. and listen to her pacing on worn floorboards in her bedroom above, the steady tapping of keys. I'd always wonder how she could stay awake all night. She often slept during the day, while we were at school, but it never seemed enough, when you looked at her. She was always tired.

Her current routine is to write during the day. Sometimes she'll start before breakfast, which usually means she ends up forgetting breakfast altogether. Other days, she'll come downstairs for a coffee and a cigarette on the back step first. That's usually when she sees us, catches us heading to school in unironed uniforms, notices Morgan has dyed her hair again, reminds us that we've forgotten chores.

This week, though, she's been sleeping in, and by the time I finish my breakfast she still hasn't come downstairs. Lauren is still asleep, I suppose—her bedroom door is shut. I wonder if Mum even knows she's back.

Morgan is in the kitchen, putting salad onto a chicken sandwich, arranging the pieces as if she's creating an artwork. Her bedroom floor is piled ankle-deep in dirty clothes and old school books, but she takes time with food. She wants to be either a chef or an artist, and for the moment she's both.

'Two minutes,' I warn her. We almost missed the bus yesterday.

'Yeah, yeah.'

I head upstairs to see if Mum's awake, feeling as if I should at least warn her that the prodigal is home. The curtains are drawn and the room is dark, but she's awake and sitting in her desk chair in her old green dressing gown. Her room always smells like stale smoke. I don't think she realises.

She looks up. 'What?' She doesn't get as defensive as Lauren, but she does sound irritable sometimes, as if I'm intruding somehow, because God forbid we interrupt her misery. Torture by a thousand drafts, that's what she says about writing.

'Lauren's back.'

'I know. I saw her come in last night. This morning. Whatever you call it. Anything else?'

Morgan calls me from downstairs and I escape out into the light, breathing in the fresh air on the landing. I always feel cowardly after those interactions, like I'm supposed to stand up to her somehow—fix something, I don't know what. I wonder if girls feel this way, or if they just accept things the way they are, and drift along in their own worlds.

Long ago, before my father left us, she was a more ordinary sort of mother. She took us to swimming lessons and went to parent–teacher interviews and served up dinner on time. But as our family life disintegrated, so did the punctuality and efficiency. She chose to spend more and more of her time in a fictional world. She often seemed to loathe it, but I suppose she could at least control it.

It starts to rain as we get to the bus stop. Morgan

never brings an umbrella so we huddle under mine, knowing that wet weather means more traffic, means a longer wait in the rain. It's cold, and she stands as close as she dares—I'm her *brother*, after all, and she's generally busy creating the impression that my mere existence embarrasses her.

'Did you see her?' Morgan asks, balling her hands inside her jumper sleeves.

'Lauren? Yeah. Not for long.'

'Why'd she come back?'

'Don't know.'

I'm not sure if we were really expecting her to come back. She took off so abruptly, only called home once, and didn't send a single postcard. It was like she'd finally escaped from a place she hated. Which makes me really wonder, now that she's back.

'Maybe she ran out of money,' Anthony comments, not looking up from his laptop.

'Maybe.' I'm not convinced, though. Nothing my older sister does is ever that simple.

He looks up at me, holding the laptop so I can see the screen. There's a large photo of a muddy river with pale-skinned tourists in conical hats teetering in wooden canoes. 'Vietnam for schoolies. Contiki. My brother met his girlfriend on a tour. What do you reckon?'

Anthony talks big but if a girl so much as sneezed in his direction I reckon he'd probably wet his pants in terror. Not that I can judge. My stomach knots at the prospect of heading out into a great unknown. I scan the oval in front of us, as if the expanse of muddy grass will give me answers. 'I don't have any money.' It's a lame excuse.

'Get a job. We've got a few months, you can save up enough.'

'Mum won't let me. Not during the HSC.' Another excuse. Mum probably wouldn't even notice. Lauren worked murderous hours throughout her HSC and still came third in her grade.

Anthony sighs, tapping the screen longingly with his index finger. 'Maybe I can talk Jimmy into it.'

Kierkegaard said that to venture causes anxiety, but not to venture is to lose one's self. The first time I read that I knew it was meant for me, but even knowing that isn't enough to overcome the sheer dread I start to feel at the thought of stepping out. I don't know why. I've thought about it—too much, probably, with my habit of overanalysing. Maybe because when my father left us I was permanently deprived of a sense of security. Maybe because I feel some twisted sense of obligation, as the only male in the household, to stay. Maybe I'm just a pathetic pussy.

The story about the racehorse always bothered me. A child's mind is different from an adult's. A child might dream of being great, but those are safe dreams, tucked up tightly in the future. There's an element of desperation about adult ambitions. Maybe because when they're grown up and they haven't fulfilled any of their grand ideals, they begin to feel as though time is running out on them. Bigger risks, higher stakes.

I write too. I can't help myself. But I don't let it become an obsession, all I care about. That just seems wrong. The thing I've never understood about Mum is the same thing I've never understood about the horse story. Why would you want glory if the cost is everything else?

before
after
later

Friday. Get busted doing Sudoku instead of writing up my biology prac. Mrs Williams hits the roof and the whole class gets a lecture. It takes her ten minutes to say, 'Do your work or don't come to my classroom.' Then the stupid cow keeps me in at lunch. Makes me wash out the beakers from her year eight science classes.

It's not that I'm not interested in biology. But this stuff is tame; I've known it all for years, from books and journals and websites and documentaries. Mrs Williams doesn't get that. I used to pester her to let us do more interesting stuff, like dissecting a brain, and she just got annoyed.

'We're following the syllabus.' That was her argument in total. Stupid narrow-minded bitch. Seriously.

Izzy grabs my arm as she passes me on the way out of school. 'I've got us hooked up for tonight, I'll text you the address. It's gonna be awesome.'

I never bother turning up to parties before nine or ten. Nothing happens before that, and it gives me time to say goodnight to Tash, wade through some of the homework we've got stuck with for the weekend, before getting myself organised.

Dan Stevens' brother is minding a house down in Coogee. Compared to Terry and Rose-Marie's every house seems big, of course, but this one is genuinely huge. Only a street or two back from the beach. A white mountain alive with people and energy.

When I get there the party's in full swing. Light and sound pulse from a hired jukebox. Must be at least a hundred people. I recognise maybe a quarter of them, most from last year's year twelve. Izzy sees me as I enter. Rushes over to grab my arm. 'You look *hot*. Damn, I wish I was Asian, look at that little size-six butt.'

'Half Asian.' Presumably. Going by the mix of features. I mean it's not like I actually *know* I'm a half-caste mongrel. Half-caste. Mongrel.

'You got the good stuff, though.' She tugs my arm. 'Come into the kitchen.'

Hot and tightly packed with people and laughter and

talking. We squeeze our way through, not bothering to apologise. Score a few glances, the sort that travel up and down your whole body before they get to your face. One guy in particular, lounging against the wall with a beer. Doesn't look away when I look back, eyebrow raised. Tall, too built to still be in school. Twenty at least and pretty good looking. I make a mental note and move on, feeling his eyes on the back of my legs as I follow Izzy into the kitchen.

Somebody's tried freezing vodka inside a watermelon and it's turned into a pink vodka slushie. I down a few shots and then follow Izzy outside.

This is what Izzy lives for; she's the biggest slut I know. She'll easily hook up with at least two different guys before the end of the night, and considers it her job to make sure I'm likewise provided for. 'Not that you really need any help, looking like that,' she whispers in my ear.

There's a slight breeze coming off the ocean, sharp and cool. It plays on my bare back, arms and legs while I make small talk. Let a few guys chat me up. I know what they want. But it gets cold, and Izzy's busy with some guy's tongue down her throat. I slip away unnoticed, back inside, where the lights are still strobing. The vodka's hit me and I take careful steps. Don't want to stack it in heels, don't want to wobble like a drunk. Squeeze through the crowd in the main living area, everything loud, flashing, moving. Looking for somebody I know. Another huge room, but quieter. Away from the jukebox, calmer without the lights. It's well decorated, expensive, but impersonal. Rose-Marie's taste. Potpourri. Rose-Marie-pot-pourri. God, I sound off my face already.

'Hey.'

The guy from before. Still easy and confident. Comes up to me and sticks out his hand. 'Nick.'

As I shake it I know exactly what I'm signing up for. 'Eliat.'

'Elliot?'

I spell it for him. He nods and fetches us both a beer. Touches my hand as he passes it to me.

'You're freezing.'

'I was outside.'

'Did you bring a jacket?'

'I'll be right.'

It gives him an excuse to shift closer, anyway. Small talk for a few minutes, movies and music. I play along. It doesn't take much thought. It always pans out pretty much the same. He gestures to the group in the corner passing joints. Hand at the small of my back, fingers hot on my skin. Gentle nudge forwards. 'Come check it out.'

The potheads are giggling. Nick takes the jay as it comes around and inhales. Offers it to me with a grin.

God, how unoriginal. I ignore the offer and reach out to the centre of the circle and draw the baggie and box of roll-your-owns closer. Cool and deliberate, like I don't know everybody's eyes are on me. Pack, roll and seal, quick and methodical. Look up. 'Lighter?'

One-handed catch and the flame flares up with a single flick. Good thing I've done this so many times, because my head is swirling like a vodka slushie machine. Steady. Let it catch properly. Take a good hit and pass it on.

Nick takes it and grins. 'Impressive.'

I shrug. 'Not exactly rocket science.'

'Where'd you learn that?'

Jesse O'Sullivan taught me in the Applebys' back shed when I was thirteen. That was where he kept his stash. We sat on piles of old hessian sacks and he ended up totally off his face and told me things too horrible to comprehend. Don't know why I kept going back in there. I didn't have anything better to do, I guess.

I arch an eyebrow. Meet Nick's gaze. 'Does it matter?'

Shrugs. 'Not to me.' Leans in closer, breath hot on my face. Hand on my back, thumbing under the edge of my dress. Whispers into my ear.

I don't do this, like Izzy does, for a tally to boast about. I do it because the roar of whatever it is—adrenaline, hormones—is enough to shut everything else up for a while.

Now the lights are back on, and we avoid eye contact as we dress. It's a much more awkward and protracted process.

I'm always clear-headed afterwards. Doesn't matter how wasted I was. I'm clear-headed and a bit empty, too. Like no matter how good it was, it's never enough, it never lasts.

'Going back out there?' He's brisk. More business-like than before.

I've already checked the time on the bedside table. Just past midnight. Early, really. 'Nah, I'm done for the night.'

'Want a lift home?'

Shake my head. 'I'll get a taxi.' Pause with my hand on the doorknob. Glance back casually. 'Thanks for warming me up.'

Terry, or maybe Rose-Marie, left the kitchen light on for me. It's too bright. Bounces off the marble and glass surfaces. I pull out the Froot Loops and sit on the bar stool to eat them. Stare at Tash's drawings on the fridge. She's starting to make things you can recognise instead of just scribbles. She can do a T for Tash now. Cute kid. Pain, though. Never shuts up.

I shut myself in my bathroom and peel off my clothes. Two late vodka shots I did on the way out collide with the Froot Loops in my stomach and I upend it all into the toilet. A multicoloured mess stinking of alcohol. Sit under the shower for twenty minutes, eyes closed in the hot spray and steam.

My eyeliner's run, I look like Halloween. I grab a

wipe and stare at my reflection for a long minute. He wasn't the biggest jerk ever. Just another guy. I still hate him, though. Among others.

Tash is asleep. Watching her, part of me wishes she was awake just for the company. In my own bed I roll straight onto my side and my mind starts to play through the usual routine. Being a show-off with the pot. Taste of watermelon vodka. A stranger's hands on me. My face in the mirror.

I clamp my eyes closed, will the memories away, and search for something else to replace them. It gets harder every time.

'You're late,' he teases. Stands up as I approach his table. I was wide awake last night worrying that I wouldn't recognise him but I do, straight away. He's immediately familiar even though I don't think I saw him smile last time. His hair is cut shorter but his eyes are the same.

'Sorry. Left my walking stick at home.'

With Mum and Alan I feel awkward talking about my leg—guilty, somehow. If they had their way I'd be scooting around in one of those motorised wheelchairs so my leg never had to take any weight. I'd never dare make that sort of smart crack with them. Mum'd blow her fuse.

He sits down opposite me. 'How is the leg?'

'Getting better. The scar's pretty epic.' I raise my left

leg, prop my foot on the edge of his chair and pull up my jeans to show my calf. It's been over a week since I shaved my legs but if regrowth ever bothered me, it doesn't now. There's been too many strangers pulling, prodding and examining this leg for me to have any shyness left, at least with anyone I'm not related to.

I love how Daniel reacts. He doesn't wince, he's just interested. I watch his eyes assess the longer scar, trace the bumps that mark the stitches. I know his doctor's eyes are looking at how neat it is. How well it's healing and all that. But there's an added element to it, beyond the professional detachment. He's remembering how it looked before.

'Tidy work.'

I grab his hand and press it against my leg where the surgeon put the metal plates in. 'Feel that?'

He prods gently, obedient. 'How long till you get them out?'

'Next year, probably.'

'Your surgeon did an excellent job.'

'I got the guy who works with the AIS, on all the Olympians.'

'Only the best for you, hey?'

'Exactly.' I push the jeans leg back down. 'I was lucky.'

A grimace flits across his face. I know he's remembering how I looked then. The way my shattered fibula had broken through my skin. The translucent flaps of

48

skin, vibrant red of my blood. And Robbie, of course.

'Lucky?' he echoes.

'Not a word you'd use?'

'Probably not.' He changes the subject. 'How come you walked here?'

'I didn't tell my parents I was meeting you. I didn't know what they'd think of the idea, so...'

He nods, slides the menu across the table at me. 'What do you want?'

We're only a few minutes from my house. This is where I used to meet up with some of my friends, so I know the menu pretty well.

'I'll have a banana cinnamon smoothie.'

He wrinkles his nose. 'Really?'

'Don't knock it till you've tried it.'

I watch him scan the list. It's been nearly a year, but I still have the sense of connection. There's none of that awkwardness that I have with the kids at my new school. Even Mum and Alan, at times. I feel safe. Bold enough to be my brutally honest, curious self.

'Do you ever think about it?'

He looks up at me, realising we've detoured off the path of easy banter. He opens his mouth to answer, then closes it again. The waitress wants to take our order.

I let him do the honours and it's only when the waitress has gone that he answers.

'Yeah. I do.'

'A lot?'

He shrugs. 'Every once in a while. When things remind me. People. Patients.'

It rained that night. Absolutely poured. We'd been in the worst drought in a hundred years and it ended that night, with so much rain that half the city flooded. There were blackouts right across Sydney, and by the time they got me into the ambulance the traffic was chaotic, lights out everywhere. It was a spectacular storm, with thunder and lightning and hail. Those are the things that remind me, now. Dark clouds in the sky make my stomach knot just that little bit.

I change the topic. 'Do you have a girlfriend?'

He smiles at the sudden shift. 'No.'

'Why not?'

A cocked eyebrow. 'Do I need a reason?'

I shrug, smile a teasing smile. 'I'd say a high percentage of high school girls would classify you as pretty hot.'

He laughs at that. 'Just what I want, a bunch of high school groupies.' Then, more seriously, 'I was in a relationship. We ended it last May.'

May. 'Before or after...?'

'That night. After I put you in the ambulance.'

'Why?'

A pause. 'It had to end. We both knew that. I guess what happened just gave me the push I needed.'

'You're welcome.' There's irony in my voice, but I don't mean it unkindly, and I know he knows that. I bite my lip, but the curiosity gets the better of me. 'What was she like?'

The question surprises him. I guess he doesn't exactly get interrogated by high school girls every day. He thinks about it for a while before answering.

'She was stubborn.' He smiles at the thought. 'You've never met a more stubborn person in your life. She was the "I don't need anybody's help" girl.'

'How did you meet?'

He raises an eyebrow. 'You really want to know?'

'Why not?' I haven't ever had a boyfriend, but it's not like I have no interest in learning how these things work. I need romance in my life as much as the next person, even if it's vicarious.

He thinks again. 'I was overseas, in the Philippines. I was in an internet cafe in Manila one day and she came in. We started chatting, just two Aussies catching up. I took her around the place to show her some things. She was studying medicine at uni, so we had a lot in common. She wanted to work with Doctors Without Borders, asked me all sorts of questions about it. We just kinda ended up hanging out for a couple of weeks.'

'Was she beautiful?'

He cracks a smile. 'What are you, six?'

I shrug. It was a reasonable question. He's a really good-looking guy, he wouldn't have trouble picking up a beautiful woman. I know I'm never going to get a guy like him. That's all right. Most of them are probably pretty vain anyway.

He shakes his head, still amused. 'She was…Not beautiful by any traditional definition, I suppose, but she had something about her. This energy…The most intense blue eyes you've ever seen, and when she smiled— if you could get a smile, it was always hard work—it was just…' He flushes, as if he realises what he's saying, and shakes his head. 'God, I sound like a total wanker.'

I laugh, wanting to disarm him. 'I think it's romantic.'

'Well, it was good while it lasted.'

'Did you love her?'

Another surprising question, it seems. Don't people ask this sort of stuff? Why not?

'Yeah.' Quietly, but there's no warning in his voice to back off. I wonder if he has friends or family that he tells this sort of stuff to, or if this is the first time he's actually had a chance to talk about it. Why are people always so determined to keep their emotions all bottled up? It's just stupid.

'But it didn't work?'

'Nope.'

'Why not?'

'I screwed up. I *was* screwed up. I was struggling with being me. I wasn't in a place where I could have a healthy relationship. Lauren wasn't really either.'

'That sucks.'

He laughs briefly, as though I've just made the understatement of the century. 'Yeah.' He braces himself against the edge of the table, thumbs curled over the edge of the aluminium top. Pondering. 'I would never wish what happened to you on anyone,' he says slowly.

There's obviously more coming. 'But?'

'But that night...' He stops again. He seems perturbed by what he wants to say.

'Spit it out.'

'It helped me. Somehow. It got me out of this rut I'd got myself into, out of that place I was in. You know what they say...Reminder of your own mortality and all that stuff.'

He stares at the tabletop, as if he can't look up at me. I try to read his face. Guilt? Why would he feel guilty? If saving my life made him feel better about himself, I'm not going to complain. Sometimes when I can't sleep I stare at my ceiling and wonder about the other people who were there, whether it changed them somehow too, or whether they simply walked away and forgot all about me and Robbie. I remember their faces: Daniel, the Asian girl who helped until the ambulance arrived, the ambos, even the people in the crowd. They all had that look on their faces that said, *That's terrible, but at least it didn't happen to me.*

I shrug, try to be nonchalant. 'We'll call it even.'

Our drinks arrive and I watch him tip one sugar into his coffee and stir it, wait for him to taste it before I hit him with the big one.

'Do you believe in God?'

He looks up, meeting my gaze with surprise that becomes frank curiosity. 'Why do you ask?'

I shrug. 'It's a valid question.' I swirl the straw around in my smoothie, stretch my legs out straighter under the table. My leg is starting to ache again, right on schedule. 'I think I do. I want to,' I say.

'What's stopping you?'

Another shrug. 'The usual arguments. I don't know if I'm that trusting. I look at the world and I want to believe that there's some grand designer behind it all, but...Usually it all just seems a bit too pointless. Random. Maybe existentialism is more my style.'

He raises an eyebrow. 'Existentialism? I didn't know philosophy was part of the current high school curriculum.'

'I've had a lot of time to Wikipedia in the last year.'

'Yeah, I guess you have.' He half smiles. 'So what do you think the point of it all is? What do you want to do with your life?'

I think back to the conversation I had with Robbie. Not long before it happened. Maybe only a week or two. The pair of us flopped on couches in the lounge room, cooling off in the air conditioning after playing basketball outside. He asked me that same question. I gave him the same answer:

'I want to change the world.'

'Change it how?'

'Yeah. That's the bit I'm still figuring out.'

*

He insists on dropping me home, even though it's literally only two blocks away. Mum and Alan are fighting about something, and I get caught in the crossfire.

'Where have you been?'

'I just went out for a walk.'

'By yourself?'

I keep it neutral. No need to exacerbate the situation. 'I met a friend at the cafe.'

'You walked all that way? Did Doctor Young say you're allowed to walk that sort of distance?'

'It's not that far.' Nothing compared to my walk home from school, or the distances Iago and I regularly trek. 'I'm careful. I stop and rest when I need to.'

'*Dio!*' She gestures in annoyance, throwing a glance heavenwards as if to ask God what she did to deserve such a stubborn daughter. Sharp eyes back on me, admonishing. 'You can set your recovery back months if you overdo it. The doctors have all told you that. Do you really want to have more surgeries?'

'It's fine, Mum. I'm fine.'

I escape, noticing as I do that Alan slipped away while her attention was on me.

Gnocchi for dinner. It fills me up too fast and I push it around on my plate, thinking of the conversation at the cafe, about how it felt to see him. There's nothing at all romantic about it, but it's left me with a sense of how

I felt that day, and I can't decide if it's a good or bad feeling.

Up in my room, I sit on my floor with my back against the wall and stare at my photos. A doll stuck up in a tree. A sea of multicoloured umbrellas surging down a rainy Sydney street in peak hour. A single leaf dangling by a thread of spiderweb, spinning. Robbie used to laugh at me because I was always holding people up, stopping to get photos of some random thing that caught my eye. If we were running late to get somewhere, my camera and I were usually to blame.

Iago follows me in, snuffling at a pile of dirty clothes. I probably got chocolate on something. I usually do. I click my tongue, calling him to me, and he waddles over, grinning that drippy, droopy grin. We sit for a long while, me staring at the photos and scratching behind his ears.

'I don't know what to do.'

It's a meaningless sentence, but it's all that comes out. It's like I've stumbled and fallen in a race and I just don't know how to get back up again, and inside me there's some sort of battle going on.

Iago just looks up at me, and I wonder what he thinks of me, whether he has an opinion at all.

It's still early when Alan pokes his head in. He looks surprised to find me in bed, but not really. I like my bed, it's my safe place.

'You all right?'

'I don't know.' It's not hard to be honest with Alan. There are times when I'm probably too honest with him. Sometimes he gets stuck in the middle between me and Mum, and I think I should keep my big mouth shut for his sake. But he's also the only one I have to talk to now.

'I left school at recess yesterday.'

'Why?'

'Just seemed like too much to handle. I didn't do anything…just came home. Took Iago for a walk. Don't tell Mum, okay?'

He smiles that same sad smile I seem to get from everyone, as if they think we're not allowed to be happy. 'About skipping school or walking Iago?'

'Both.'

He nods. 'Okay.'

I think back to earlier when he and Mum were fighting. It seems to be getting more frequent.

'What's Mum mad at you about?'

'I wish I knew.'

'You should take her out for dinner or something.'

'She's busy.'

She's been busy since Robbie. It doesn't take a psychoanalyst to see the connection. She just keeps taking on new clients and then all she can talk about is how busy she is.

'Let's go on a holiday or something, then.'

57

'She won't take a night off. You really think you'll get her on an aeroplane?'

'True.' I consider him for a moment. I've never had problems asking people the tough questions, or wanting to talk about the important stuff, but sometimes there's no point. Sometimes there's no answer, and all you're doing is stirring up grief. This might be one of those areas.

'Does she ever talk to you?'

He shrugs.

'Maybe you should talk to her.'

'It's not as easy as that. We don't all have...'

'My big mouth?'

He smiles. 'You get away with asking those sorts of question. I can do it at work. Here is different. And lately...it's a bit hard.'

'You should just take her away. Call her work and get them to cancel all her appointments and take her somewhere. Italy, France...Tasmania—who cares? Just get her away from all her excuses.'

'She'd kill me.'

'Yeah, but once she's done with that she might actually unwind enough to have a conversation.'

'Maybe.' He looks around, sees my canvases stacked against the wall.

'You haven't done much painting lately.'

I laugh. I don't want him to think it's a big deal. 'No time in my hectic social calendar.'

I remember the day that my father left us. He would probably argue that it was Mum that he left, not us, but the end result was the same.

Lauren and I did swimming lessons at an indoor pool only a few streets away. Mum had dropped us off as usual—back then nobody had even heard the term 'helicopter parent'—and Lauren's lesson usually finished ten minutes before mine, meaning she had to wait for me. My sister has never been a patient person, least of all with me.

She was standing at the end of the pool as I hoisted myself out, with my towel over her shoulder and my clothes bundled in her arms. 'Hurry up, stupid.' She threw the towel at me and it hit the ground, landing in a puddle that had formed at my feet.

'C'mon, dork.' She grabbed my arm.

Her thongs flip-flopped across the hard floor, splashing up the puddles so that by the time we reached the exit my legs were dripping again. We stood in the carpark and I shivered in the cold breeze that swept through. No Mum.

When Lauren let go of my arm, it was splotched red, but I didn't say anything. I drew my soggy towel around my shoulders and tried to ignore the anxious butterflies in my stomach.

Lauren didn't seem concerned or particularly impatient—at least, no more than usual. She practised her tightrope walking along the edge of the gutter, shredded the leaves on the banana tree behind us and watched as the wind whisked the fragments away.

My mind whirled. Stories of little lost children; Mum lying dead, murdered in our house, eaten by some unimaginable creature or crushed to bits in a car accident. A flurry of panic rising in my chest like breath.

We waited as the sky grew darker. Lauren stopped playing and stood still, tensed. The carpark emptied slowly and the buzz of kid chatter died down.

Pressed by all the nightmare possibilities, my mind weighed and rejected appeals to Lauren. Weighed and rejected. I swallowed them back one at a time, they would sound stupid and babyish.

We waited. Then, at last, a glimpse of white. The sound of a labouring V8, and our white station wagon rumbled down the unguttered driveway. Mum pulled up and leaned *over to swing the passenger door open. 'I know I'm late. Get in before the storm breaks.'*

I lurched, grabbed the doorhandle, yanking it open. Morgan was in her childseat in the back, chubby face stained with tears. I climbed in beside her, belting myself in the middle, waiting for Lauren to climb up beside me, but she stood outside, arms folded.

'In the car, Lauren.' Mum sounded impatient, angrier than usual at the disobedience. I felt my heart sink again when I realised my sister was not going to make this easy.

'Lauren Elizabeth McAlpine...' More than just the normal amount of tired. Her voice was wobbly, like she was trying not to cry.

Lauren stood fast and refused even to look in our mother's direction. Mum turned off the engine, jumped out of the car and strode around to Lauren's side. Her right hand hovered as if she wanted to slap my sister.

'You've got three seconds.'

The tone wasn't one to be messed with, and Lauren flinched. But she wouldn't give in. Mum slammed the door, furious. Stormed back around, climbed in, restarted the engine. Yanking the handbrake so hard I was afraid she'd break something. She accelerated, the car lurched and we skidded in the gravel before the tyres regained their grip and Mum pulled a sharp U-turn in the near-empty carpark. Facing towards the road, she stopped.

My heart was pounding like before, but worse. My mother hadn't been eaten by a monster, she seemed to have

*become one. I couldn't see Lauren properly past Morgan's car
seat, and if I leaned past her to look, my squirming would
only provoke my mother further. I was sure my mother was
going to drive off, leaving my sister alone in the dark.*

*I thought my heart was about to burst from apprehen-
sion when I heard the doorhandle. The door swung open;
Lauren climbed in. Silent, her face dark as the sky outside,
not looking at any of us as she drew her seatbelt on and
the door closed. A trickle of blood meandered down the
outside of her right leg. A piece of gravel, kicked up by the
car wheels. She saw me staring and pinched my arm: say
nothing. I looked at the fierce anger in those frightening
eyes. I shut my mouth.*

*We drove home in silence to an empty house. Neither
Lauren nor I questioned our father's sudden absence or the
now-empty spaces in wardrobes and shoe racks and closets.
We just knew, somehow, and we knew better than to say
a word.*

'What do you mean, *out*?'

I stare at my sister, hands on my hips as I try to catch
my breath. Mum doesn't just go out. Mum hasn't left
the house in over a month. And it's a Saturday morning.

She shrugs. 'She didn't say. I assume she's meeting
her editor or something. She's an adult; she can do what
she wants.'

This irritating answer typifies Lauren's opinion that
people should take responsibility for themselves and

mind their own business. She moves around the kitchen pulling out rolled oats, milk and a saucepan. 'Have you had breakfast?'

'I went for a run.'

'You're stupid to skip breakfast.'

'I'm not skipping breakfast.' I always feel like I'm on the defensive with Lauren. Something about her manner just makes me feel small, immature, naive. *All boys are idiots*, I can still hear her seven-year-old voice informing me, *especially you.*

'I'm just not hungry.' I'm waiting for her to get angry at me, to tell me how selfish or stupid I am, but she doesn't.

'I'll make you some porridge.' Her voice is level, immune to provocation. She pulls out the juicer, a chopping board and knife and a couple of oranges. 'Make yourself useful.'

This isn't the Lauren I know. The Lauren I know would take this opportunity to cut me down. Scathing criticism, sarcasm; some cruel, biting comment. Where's the angry, impatient confidence? She's still on her guard, not giving an inch, but the fire is gone.

I start to cut the oranges. I'm wary. I always am with her. I know when we were kids there were plenty of moments of comradeship. Building forts inside on rainy days. Summers with the slip-n-slide, pouring on dishwashing detergent until the backyard was a snowfield of white bubbles. I don't know when we became strangers to each other. Maybe it was easier when we were kids to forget the things that hurt, to let each day start afresh. Maybe it was when we got old enough to realise I was the odd one out. I wonder all the time if my sisters are disappointed that I didn't turn out like all the other guys, big and muscled and dumb. Would Lauren still treat me with contempt if I had grown taller than her? Or is it just her personality to find fault no matter what?

We set things down on the kitchen table to eat. Lauren looks around. 'Did we get the paper?'

What she's really asking is where it is. We've had the paper delivered for as long as I can remember. Dad was pedantic about reading it every morning before work, and after the divorce for some reason Mum never stopped the subscription. For a couple of years it wasn't used for much more than papier-mache and occasionally newspaper hockey in the house, until eleven-year-old Lauren started taking an interest in the headlines, and from that point on we never heard the end of it. Our own problems were relegated to irrelevancies as we were force-fed stats of the state of the world.

'Do you know how lucky we are?' That was what she always said. Then a list of horrible deprivations. 'Preventable blindness, malnutrition, illiteracy…'

Now I say quietly, still expecting her to explode at any moment, 'Out the front.'

She fetches it and pushes her breakfast aside to unroll it on the table. Smooths it out and scans the headlines, then pushes the whole thing away from her, and says quietly, 'Nothing ever really changes...'

She seems changed, though. Defeated somehow. I don't know what to say. I want to ask her what happened to her while she was gone, what's done this to her, but I don't dare.

Lauren's always been the fearless one in the family, not just fighting the battles that came our way but sometimes going out of hers to pick them. And Morgan was always brave too, the little three-year-old we'd drag around the neighbourhood when we were knocking on doors selling raffle tickets. Lauren and I would hang back and let Morgan charm them with her big grin, her easy love. Me, I'm the one who should be the bravest and isn't. The one who stays quiet because I can't summon the courage to ask, who accepts injustice because I'm too scared to stand up for myself. I'm still that kid with the sopping wet towel, keeping my mouth shut and letting others rule me.

before
after
later

The zoo is packed and Tash is arking up, refusing to sit in the stroller anymore. Terry and I take turns carrying her on our shoulders. Rose-Marie is like a whirlwind with her digital camera, not just endless photos but video, too. Photos are bad, but I really hate video. That feeling of being captured. Hard to say no to Rose-Marie, though. She's more excited about this outing than Tash.

I'm not hungover but it's a hot day for March. The sun's giving me a throbbing headache. We stick to the shady side of the path but even then the light sneaks through the gaps in the foliage, a strobing on my retinas. I leave the others looking at the zebras and go throw up in the toilets, hoping it will make the pulsing pain go away.

*

Home at two for Tash's afternoon nap, and Rose-Marie and Terry are packing. They're heading to the Hunter Valley to spend tonight and Sunday at a winery. Terry's been watching the weather up there for weeks to pick the perfect weekend. I think he's planning on surprising her with a hot air balloon ride. Rich people have money to waste on shit like that.

It takes forty minutes to convince them we'll be fine without them. I actually give Terry a push out the door.

'Go now or I really will finish off the coffee.'

I'm not stupid enough to do anything at the house; I do exactly what I told Terry I'd do, which is put Tash to bed on time and sit down to do my *Othello* essay. Go for the rum and Coke, though, not coffee, reading and rereading pages of Shakespeare that won't sink in. There's a panicky edge to the feeling of not-understanding that just makes it worse.

I push the Coke away, reach for the bottle and take a couple of good pulls. The burn spreads through me, relaxes me a little. Forget the text then, I'll just get straight into the essay. Haven't got the focus for a structured job like usual. Maybe something will just flow.

It's just past eleven when I make it to a thousand words, helped out by regular hits from the bottle. Tired eyes, words starting to blur. A coffee would keep me going but it gets me wired too, and on top of the rum

I'll end up not knowing which way is up.

Save document. Crawl onto bed. Just a nap.

'Hello?' Baby breath on my face and a tugging on my ears. Tash. Open my eyes to find her right up in my face, big eyes on me. She pushes a book into my face, one of those touch and feel books, different textures and bits of fabric on each page. Rose-Marie bought it for her at the zoo.

'Not now.' I brush the book aside and pull myself upright. My head lurches in protest. The laptop's gone to sleep. I want to go back to sleep.

Think straight, Eliat. What would Rose-Marie say? 'It's past your bedtime.'

'Whatchu doing?'

'I'm working on an assignment for school. I have to get it done, so you have to go back to bed now. Okay?'

'Have to read.'

'No, we already read that one, when I put you to bed. Do you want me to tell Rose-Marie you wouldn't go to sleep?'

She frowns, and I shift her off me before she can complain anymore. 'C'mon, I'll beat you back to your bedroom.'

Takes me half an hour to get her back to sleep. I have to sit patting her stomach, trying to get her to lie still. Fighting to keep myself awake.

Back to my bedroom, too brightly lit after sitting in the dark with only a twinkling blue nightlight. Reach to switch the ceiling light off so I can work in the dark. Pause.

The Coke can's on its side. There's a dark brown puddle on the floor in front of my desk. I didn't...Ah, shit. Tash.

I can't tell whether she actually managed to drink any of it before she knocked it over. She's sound asleep on her back, breathing normally, and I let out a breath I didn't even know I was holding. What was I expecting, to find her dancing drunkenly on her bed? Maybe. I sit there for a long minute, waiting, waiting. Nothing changes.

I clean up and crawl into bed. Stare at the glowing red digits on my alarm clock, mind buzzing tiredly. The scare with Tash has got my adrenaline pumping. No chance of sleep now.

This is when the demons come out, when everything comes back. The things I've done. Somehow worse, the things I've heard and seen. Stories I heard about other kids in foster care. Kids who'd wet the bed every night or freak out if you tried to make them sleep in the dark. Screwed-up kids.

Tash is snoring. I don't care. I scoop her up and shift her over. There's just room enough for us both and she stirs, but resettles without waking.

*

Sunday. I have to rewrite most of my essay. Tash gets a Disney marathon and her musical Hi-5 playmat while I sit at the kitchen counter with earplugs. No other way I can tolerate three continuous hours of the playmat, let alone get any actual work done.

Still a hard grind, though. Every time I manage to get my thoughts on track Tash has another question, or she wants food or attention. When everything but the conclusion's done I call it a day. Spend the next twenty minutes tidying up the trail of Duplo and zoo animals Tash's left right through the house.

When Terry and Rose-Marie get home I hand her over and say I'm going out.

'Where?'

No stress. They love their little weekends away, always come back calmer. It's a prime time to push the boundary just that little bit.

'Movies with April. I think her boyfriend might be coming too, and some other people…Seven o'clock session, I'll be home by ten.'

Sunday night is Sober Night, some vague group attempt at responsible behaviour. Doesn't stop Jade and Mel from singing along to the radio all the way; it just means they've got no excuse for sounding so shit. Of course, it's less than fifteen hours since their Saturday night wrapped up, so it's possible they're still technically intoxicated. After the singing come the dares. Streaking in public places is always popular.

'Remember the time Izzy did it on the freeway?'

'You should do it on the bridge.'

'Which bridge?'

'*The* bridge.'

'What about the tourists?'

'So do it at three in the morning.'

Stop at Macca's for thirty-cent cones. Not in the mood. I sit and scan the newspaper while they giggle, a bit bored. It all just gets old after a while.

'Don't you guys ever get sick of this?'

'Of what?'

'Doing the same thing all the time...soft-serve cones on Sundays, pot and kebabs on Saturdays...'

They stare at me. The idea has never occurred to them. I can picture them still sitting here this time next year, in four or five years' time, still loving it. The thought of even six more months in this place makes me feel claustrophobic.

I've been with Terry and Rose-Marie for just over two years. Only ever stayed in one place longer than that. The McIntyres, from when I was eight till just after I turned eleven. Still remember that restlessness, as if my patience with them, their family, their life, had run out.

I get April to drop me off at the petrol station and I take the shortcut through the lane. Stop and sit in the gutter outside the terrace house. There's something so perfect about it, the paint job and the cutesy old-fashioned iron railings. I know exactly what I'm coming home to: Rose-Marie in the bathroom getting ready for bed. Her ridiculously casually expensive beauty regime. I've met her parents, been to the house she grew up in. She's never had to worry about money in her life. Never had to worry about where she might be sleeping the next night. Must be easy to be nice, to be generous to people, when it's the only way you've ever been treated.

Terry is watching the late-night news with his feet up on the coffee table because Rose-Marie isn't there to tell him off. Knowing these things should make me feel safe. They just make me impatient.

I used to think I'd move to the city and finally be free. Thought the whole idea of a city was that nobody knew you, nobody cared what you were doing; you could just get lost in the crowd. Turns out to be just as much pressure to toe the line. Only difference is there's more noise and fewer stars.

before
after
later

In art, Wednesdays are theory lessons. This school is even worse than my old one for looking at artworks as if we're in primary school. What's the name? Who was the artist? When was it made? Conceptual framework, frames, blah blah. Either you get art or you don't. Either it makes you catch your breath or it doesn't. I don't think people can be taught to understand it. Not like this, anyway. So I tune out, scribbling down the notes in my unreadable handwriting without even caring what I'm writing.

I used to want my art to be a splash. Throwing myself on the world's mercy. Challenging them to see me, love me or hate me. I wanted to paint as if my life depended on it. I wanted people to look at it and say, 'Wow, that's one really screwed-up girl' or 'Damn, that's deep', not just write down the title and my name and dates. I used to think I was the only one who felt anything. Now I'm not feeling it either.

The bell goes and Sarah Bancroft trips on my bag on her way out. A minor stumble, no faceplant or anything embarrassing. But she straightens up, fixes her hair, and throws me a cold, dirty look. 'Your bag is in the way.'

I've seen other students in the grade take crap from her royal highness. I'm not interested in it. If she wants to hate my guts, so be it. And part of me is hanging out for a good fight. 'Maybe you should look where you're going.'

The ice queen just stares at me, loathing me, and walks out. What is it with people who think they're gorgeous and hate anybody who isn't?

I run into Morgan outside, waiting in the bus bay. We've shared the darkroom a couple of times now, but this is the first time I've seen her properly out in the light. And the first time she's seen me.

It's always interesting to watch people's reactions to my leg. Some people notice, then get embarrassed and pretend that they haven't. Others are totally tactless. Morgan's eyes are lit up with curiosity. 'Whoa, cool scar. Where's it from?'

'I was in an accident.'

'Like a car accident?'

'Yeah.'

'That's huge.' She lifts her arm up to show me a long-faded streak across her elbow. 'Lauren—my sister—threw a paperweight at me when I was four. Ten stitches. I don't really remember it, though. She's a bit psycho sometimes.'

Seeing Morgan properly in the light, I can see why I feel so comfortable with her. We could pass as sisters, though I'm at least half a foot taller than her. She has messy hair, scuffed school shoes, and she's painted her fingernails black; they match mine.

She points to my wristbands. Mum hates them, especially the studs. 'I like your wristbands.'

She has a naivety that makes me smile, though it reminds me of Robbie. 'Thanks.'

My bus rolls up. Fifty kids run for the door, pushing and shoving, and I wait and watch it happen, not bothered. I don't care if I have to stand the twenty minutes home. I'm not interested in getting the back seat or who I end up sitting next to. Turns out life's just easier that way.

I indicate. 'You catching the bus?' It's the last one, I learned that the hard way.

Morgan shakes her head. 'I was going to hang out with a friend.' She looks around, as if just starting to realise. 'Think she's forgotten…'

'How are you getting home?'

A shrug, nonplussed. 'I'll figure it out.'

Her attitude kicks off the big-sister spontaneity in me. Robbie and I did it all the time, mostly out of pure competitiveness. Dare you to talk to the guard in the big furry hat. Race you round the Colosseum. The Colosseum turned out to be much bigger than it looks.

'The Archibalds just opened at the gallery. You wanna go check them out?' I half shrug, as if it's no big deal.

A grin, as if I've just offered her a treat. 'Really?'

'Yeah. Wednesdays is Art After Hours. We have to walk to the train station, though.' My bus goes the opposite direction.

'I know a shortcut.'

The shortcut involves back alleys and carparks, then jumping the fence of the local pub. Morgan sets a cracking pace, talking the whole time, and not turning back once to check I'm okay. My leg is hurting almost from the start but I don't tell her. Her not knowing makes it not real. It's liberating being with somebody who doesn't think to fuss.

The last hundred metres is a sprint along the platform and into a waiting carriage just before the doors slide shut. It's already packed with kids in different uniforms and we squeeze into a space against the doors, trying to catch our breath.

Morgan uncurls her hand to show me a brilliant green leaf, crushed a little by her grip, snagged on the way.

'I love these leaves. Look at the green. Doesn't that make you think of summer?'

For a moment I forget the pain, forget that I'm out of breath, and just smile.

Neither of us has the entry fee so we have to sneak in when the attendant isn't looking. It turns out Morgan's a voluble art critic, worse than me. She analyses each image as we pass it, passing over the more traditional-style portraits for the brightly coloured ones and throwing about artists' names.

'That's *so* Morimura, what a rip-off…Hey, doesn't that one there make you think of Charles Blackman? The brushstrokes…'

Afterwards, we walk back to St James, hop a City Circle train to Wynyard, then squeeze onto a North Shore train. It's still peak hour coming home from the city and there's no seats, but the jam of people helps keep me propped upright. I hang onto the pole and try to keep my weight off my leg as much as possible.

Morgan gets off a few stops before me. She reckons her house is only a five-minute walk from the station and it's still light outside so I figure she'll be fine. I'm not so lucky. It's at least a ten-minute drive home from the station—an hour's walk at best, and probably twice that with my leg hurting. Hopefully I can get Alan to pick me up.

Part of me feels tired all of a sudden, but it's a satisfied tiredness. I didn't think about Robbie, or Mum, or school, for at least two hours. In that space, I felt like nothing had changed.

I pull my phone out to call home. I switched it off in the gallery, because I've got into trouble before, but also…Also because even though I don't have friends who constantly call and text message all day, there's still something defining about shutting it off, making myself unreachable.

Six messages. Two from Alan, the rest telling me I have missed calls.

Where are you? Don't forget dinner.

Call me ASAP.

Shit. My stomach takes a dive. Mum's three-months-late new year's dinner…

I call Alan.

'Where are you?' He sounds calm. In the background I can hear a raucous cry in Italian, not my mother's.

Guests are already arriving. I'm dead.

'I'm on the train. I went into the art gallery, with a friend, to see the Archibalds…I forgot…Is Mum mad?'

He doesn't answer that; just says he'll meet me at the station.

I'm sitting on the edge of the footpath, leg stretched out in front of me, when he rolls up. The four-wheel drives are impossible to get into one-legged. I step up, gritting my teeth as I put weight on my leg, not wanting to be more of a nuisance by needing help.

'What did you tell Mum?'

'She thinks you had a physio appointment.'

'I'll need one.'

Alan has lied for me before, but usually little stuff, like saying it was him who knocked the bit of tile off the antique mosaic coffee table. Funny, because he's such a straight arrow. He must have figured out long ago it was better to appease Mum than tell her the truth.

'Didn't she wonder why it's so late?'

'She's busy with dinner. You got lucky.'

I try to stretch my leg out, try to massage the cramp out. 'Sorry you're missing the party.'

He smiles at that. An actual smile, because we both know how much he hates Mum's 'Italian affairs'.

I manage a smile back. 'You can thank me later.'

Sunday morning dawns bright, dew on the grass. I'm up early to go for a run, and I find Mum out on the front steps in her dressing gown, toying with an unlit cigarette. She was pacing most of the night—her footsteps above kept waking me up. I study her in the way a meteorologist might study the sky. Scanning for approaching storms. I don't consciously set out to analyse her mood; it's just something I've learned to do because it's useful to know what I'm dealing with.

'How is your book going?'

She doesn't answer at first.

'I'm in the "depths of despair",' she says finally. She gives me a quick, wry smile. It only takes me a second to place the melodramatic phrase and I smile too. But it's a careful smile, one that remembers the times she's been so engulfed by depression we haven't seen her for days on end.

She taps the cigarette lightly against her knee. 'Do you remember how I used to read *Anne of Green Gables* to you every night before bed? You loved those books until Lauren told you they were for girls, then you refused to have them anymore.'

I suppose that's something I have to thank my sister for. It had just never occurred to me that boys shouldn't be reading stories about girls. I don't know if I would have ever worked that out without her. I just loved books. I loved characters and places that came alive, and it didn't really make much difference whether they were boys or girls or alien superheroes.

'I used to read those same stories when I was younger. Before you were born I thought you were going to be another girl. I wanted to call you Anne.'

I nod, awkward. What does she really expect me to say to that?

In the early days of Mum's writing she would be hidden in her room for days on end. We'd hear her footsteps and the clicking of typewriter keys, day and night. After her first book got published, when I was nine, it became more sporadic. She'd achieved some level of success, but I guess she was becoming disillusioned with the process. She seemed to write less. To spend just as much time reading or sitting upstairs, thinking. She took to coming downstairs more often, too. If she found me alone she'd always stop to talk to me. It was odd in a way, none of us were used to just chatting with our mother. I felt she must have thought of me as an ally or a protégé, maybe both. I wrote more, and though it was done in shame and secret in my bedroom, never shared with anybody, somehow Mum seemed to know.

'I know you do it too,' she mused one day. 'You see the way light comes through a window, and you find yourself searching for a word to describe it, that *is* it… You understand that words are beautiful.'

I read, too. Mostly I reread all my old books. Mum's never offered to buy me any new ones and I have a surprising aversion to libraries. I don't like the idea of reading something that doesn't belong to me. Books are personal, too personal to just borrow and share. I'd sooner lend out every other possession I own than a single one of my books.

Her moods were always up and down. About six months after her first book was published they reached a new low. One afternoon, I got home from school and ventured upstairs to ask for money for an excursion, to find her still in bed.

It wasn't a good sort of still-in-bed. She wasn't just having one of those days where she would put on comfy clothes or stay in her pyjamas and sit reading. It was dark in her room and the air reeked of stale cigarette smoke, and when she answered me her voice sounded dull and tired.

'Mum?'

'Not now, Will.'

I didn't know what to say then, so I left again, stopping at the bottom of the stairs to breathe in the fresh air. I could feel the sick smoky smell clinging to my clothes and hair.

'Mum's still in bed,' I told Lauren when she got home from school. She was in year seven, and her school finished half an hour after mine.

'So?'

'It's afternoon.'

'Who cares? She probably stayed all up night writing.'

I went away, not convinced by my sister's argument. All that afternoon and evening I kept expecting to hear the clicking of the typewriter start up, but it was quiet upstairs.

It went on that way for a week. Then I called Aunty Jen.

'Will! How's school?'

The bright smile didn't fool me; I could see the concern in her eyes. She was still in her work clothes, and I knew she'd rushed straight over because she normally took off her high heels the first chance she got.

'We don't have any food left in the house,' was all I said.

All three of us followed her up to the stairs, hanging out on the landing as she went in to talk to Mum.

'God, Sandra, it stinks in here. I thought you quit.'

Mum, nothing more than a bunch of shadows and blankets, murmured something and Aunt Jen forced a laugh. 'Yeah, sure.'

She came back over to the door and gestured at us to shoo. 'I'll be down in a bit.'

We sat grimly at the kitchen counter for the next hour or so, waiting for her to come down. I stared hard at a plastic orange bowl full of burnt popcorn, not wanting to speak in case I tipped the scales in some terrible way.

Lauren looked at Morgan, then at me. Her eyes were piercing, her jaw set. 'We're not going into foster care.'

I didn't ask her how she could be so sure. Somehow I just believed her: she would keep that promise, however she could.

And somehow, she did. We didn't go into foster care. Aunty Jen stayed for a month, taking over running the house. That didn't go over much better with Lauren, who was used to doing things her way. But Aunty Jen's reign, as friction-filled as some moments were, was a brief escape into my old life of packed lunches, bedtime stories and goodnight kisses. I knew it wasn't going to last forever, but I clung to each tenuous moment, trying to store up what I could.

I was sitting on the front step reading when I encountered my mother for the first time in almost two weeks. I'd fled to escape an argument between Aunty Jen and Lauren. I pulled my book close against me as I felt the front door swing inwards, expecting a violent flurry of movement and the angry strides of my sister. But it wasn't Lauren's

*tread. It was still crisp, but more careful; a little hesitant.
Mum.*

*She paused. My head was still down as I pretended to
be deep in the book, but I could hear her quiet breathing
behind me. The clipped footsteps moved past, and she
stopped a few metres away with her back to me. I could
tell from the way she searched her pockets and then cupped
her hands to her face that she was lighting a cigarette.
Finally she turned around, meeting my gaze and shuffling
a little.*

'What are you reading?'

*Her voice was surprisingly clear, casual. I'd expected
her to look different, ill somehow, but Aunty Jen had been
making her eat properly and it looked like she'd just show-
ered and washed her hair.*

*I held my book up to show her, and she raised an
eyebrow. 'You need some new stuff.' Again she shuffled,
stamping her feet as if it was really cold, and she came
forwards, reaching for the ashtray that I had nudged aside
with my feet. 'That's not challenging for you.'*

*This wasn't at all how I'd imagined this meeting would
go. I wanted to say something, to tell her how unfair she'd
been on us, but I wasn't brave enough. When I did speak,
my voice was shaky: 'Aunty Jen says...you feel like you're
letting everyone down.'*

*Mum raised an eyebrow and let out a scornful snort.
'Jen likes to think she knows what everyone feels.' She
tapped her cigarette against the rim of the ashtray. Red*

embers tumbled, curling and blackening as they died. 'But I have let you all down.'

Only when you go all weird and don't get out of bed. Only when your writing is more important to you than us.

That's what I wanted to say to her, but I didn't. I should have been the bravest, but if anything I was the biggest wuss, the last one to speak out. Lauren would explode all over the place, and even Morgan would complain, but I would just sit there silently, feeling as if my mouth had forgotten how to work.

'Come on.' She stubbed out her cigarette. 'It's time I introduce you to my classics.'

'Mum?' My voice was wobbly, nervous.

She turned back.

I felt sick in my stomach as I asked, 'Are you going to keep writing?'

She turned fully to face me. Leaned back against the wall. 'It's all I ever wanted to do.'

'More than have us?'

'It's not the same.'

'Why not?'

'It's just not. I have to write. It's in my blood. I knew I wanted to do it just like I knew I wanted you three.'

'What if you can't have both?'

That stopped her. She rubbed at her eyes. 'It's been a horrible, crazy month, Will. Go to sleep, we'll talk about it in the morning.'

*

Aunty Jen went back to her flat mid-May. I half expected everything to go pear-shaped within minutes without her around, but somehow we all just carried on. Lauren took over as boss, making sure we did our chores if Mum hadn't swept through and done them first.

I worked through the stack of Mum's classics. In the playground or on a sporting field I always felt out of place and out of my depth, but when I read I felt like I had found a second home, a place without contemptuous laughter or disappointed sighing. War and Peace *was a challenge, but even so I was inspired. My own suburban primary school life was mundane against the grandeur and drama of times and places steeped in bloody history.*

I wrote, too. I couldn't help it. Snatches of conversations would just sneak their way into my head and go round and round until I released them to paper. I never got beyond the first chapter, never really built up any of my characters. It was all terribly clichéd, full of tragic heroes, vivid descriptions of places I'd never actually been, and unbelievable dialogue. Yet, despite myself, the more I read, the more compelled I felt to write. I couldn't help myself. In year seven I spent three weeks labouring over a short story for English. My teacher entered the story into a competition for me and I won.

'Good,' was Mum's crisp response when I showed her the award, and she plied me with more books. 'You need to give Shakespeare a proper go. I'll see if I can hunt up some T.S. Eliot as well.'

It was always about books. She sometimes used to quote Kierkegaard at me. 'The whole age can be divided into those who write and those who do not.'

I used to wonder. Did she see it that way—a few of us against the world? She had withdrawn from the world, deliberately, almost as a statement that they couldn't understand her. I felt a sense of inevitable despair, knowing that I understood and shared that unquenchable need to write, but hating the thought of becoming the thing that I had loathed my whole life.

Mum stands abruptly. 'Back to work.'

Something inside me cries out for her to stop, to wait, to listen, but I don't know what I would say to her. For ten years I've been trying to find words to tell her to stop burning herself out for a worthless cause, that she's got to make a choice to give up one or the other because she can't have both, and it's nearly too late.

I do the hour-long loop, along Galbraith Gorge, then wind my way home again. I'm nearly done when I see a familiar lean figure approaching from the end of the street. Lauren. Headphones in her ears and eyes on the ground as she runs, determination on her face like she's going to push herself harder and harder even if it kills her. Across the other side of the road, she doesn't look up once. We pass each other without her noticing.

Maybe it's already too late.

Monday after recess we get our marks back on our ancient history essay. I get 45. Percent. Even the *Othello* debacle a couple of weeks back didn't end up that bad.

Mr Hensley is new to the school. I thought he seemed easy enough to get onside. Looks like I was wrong.

I go up to him at his desk and demand to know what was wrong with it. He doesn't mince words.

'It was lazy. You didn't use anywhere near enough sources, and only cited half of them, and it was too short.'

Yeah, it was. But that's the way I've always done history essays. Always got away with it. As long as it sounds impressive, most teachers can't tell the difference. The fact he's right doesn't make it any less irritating.

*

Still stewing over the essay mark at lunch time. Izzy shrugs and keeps flipping through her magazine. 'What does it matter?'

'It matters.' It's hardly surprising she doesn't understand but it still shits me.

She stops flipping and looks up at me, clearly following her own train of thought. 'Brett and the guys are going out shooting on the weekend. Killing kangaroos and stuff on his uncle's farm.' Wrinkles her nose. 'It's gross.'

I shrug. 'They're a massive problem. That's why the government gives out licences to cull them.'

I watch her eyes go wide, like I've just suggested going out and drowning a bag of kittens. She seems to have no comprehension sometimes that there's a whole rest of the country out there, let alone a world. A bit like Rose-Marie, though I can't really imagine Rose-Marie getting up to any of the stuff Izzy does on weekends. Still. They both have that clueless streak. I feel a bit sorry for them sometimes. That nice, comfortable world they live in is very small.

'I grew up in the country, Iz. I've shot stuff.'

'Oh yeah. I forgot.'

God, she's blonde. Sometimes wonder how I've put up with Izzy so long.

'Still. I can't believe he'd do it. He even asked if I wanted to go along. I mean, seriously? It's a five-hour drive each way in a car full of serious BO.' She shudders dramatically. 'I don't think so.'

Free period last so I go pick up Tash early. The kids are just finishing their afternoon snack and getting covered with sunscreen before they can go play. Tash is still sitting at the table on the verandah, a half-eaten quarter piece of Vegemite toast in one hand, picking through her bowl of fruit with the other. Pair of rabbit ears from the dress-ups box.

I hang back for a minute. Watch her eat a piece of rockmelon, then shove the rest of the toast into the same mouthful as if she's suddenly realised she's losing valuable play time.

She decides she's done with the rest of the fruit. Climbs out of her seat, wrestling it back under the table, and trots over to the hat box to find her Dorothy the Dinosaur hat. Turns around, tugging the hat sideways onto her head, on top of the rabbit ears. Sees me.

Her face is covered in Vegemite and I know her hands will be sticky from the fruit. Learned that from experience. I snag a wet wipe from the box on the shelf and go for her hands as she comes running, wiping them and her face clean before I let her grab me.

Tash always has a lot to say and tries to say it all at once. Her sentences are getting longer and longer but she hasn't quite cracked knowing when to end them. She keeps banging on when I say, 'Yeah, okay, I get it,' then chucks a tantrum when I pull the rabbit ears off. I cop a kick to the stomach as I lift her up.

'Stop it or you'll get a smack.' The way I say it, she knows I'm serious. Looks at me reproachfully, snot hanging out of one nostril. I take a tissue from the shelf and wipe her face clean again.

Dirty looks from people on the bus. It's always worse when I'm in school uniform. I meet the looks with a cold stare. Pretend to be interested in Tash's prattle as she watches out the bus window.

'Just wait. The water's yucky.' It might be April but nothing's going to quench the kid's determination to get wet. Never mind that there's a puddle of stagnant rainwater in the bottom of the wading pool that looks and smells like stale piss. I grab Tash before she can clamber in, Rose-Marie would chuck a fit if she found out.

I need a distraction. 'Go get the hose, okay? Your pool needs more water.'

I upend it while her back is turned and grimace at the stink of stagnant water and sun-warmed plastic. Turn my face away from the remnants of a squashed slug on the underside of the plastic.

'The things I do for you, kid…'

I stretch out on the deckchair and manage to get ten minutes' worth of homework done while she paddles in the refilled pool. When she climbs out the endless questions start.

'What's that?'

'My biology homework. For school. These things are called Punnett squares.'

'Pun-nit squares,' she repeats after me, as if the word actually means something to her. Reaches out for my book with wet hands, dripping onto the pages.

'No. You'll make it wet. Why don't you get back into the pool and do some swimming?'

Rose-Marie takes her to swimming lessons Friday mornings. The wading pool only has a few inches of water in it, but Tash will splash around trying to dogpaddle and 'breathe and bubble' like she does in the bath.

'Don't wanna.'

That's it then. Once she makes up her mind, she won't change it. I get her to help me tip the water out and prop the wading pool against the side of the house to drain. Wrap her up in her towel but she wriggles away when I try to dry her off, so I kick a ball with her for five minutes till she dries off a bit. We go in and I let her choose one of her DVDs to watch. 'Don't tell Rose-Marie, okay? Or we'll both get in trouble.'

Get the mail in; letter from school. It's an unmarked envelope—which means I'm in shit—but they're the only ones who refer to Rose-Marie and Terry as Mr and Mrs.

I open it up carefully in case it's something I'll need to reseal. A warning letter from Mrs Williams. Lack of sustained effort in bio. My first, and she didn't even tell me it was coming. Cow.

Grab a felt tip and dash off Terry's trademark scrawl in the acknowledgement fields. Tear off the bottom section, seal it up in the return envelope, hide it in my school bag. The rest of the letter I shred and then flush. Call Izzy.

'Can we do something tonight?' She knows how to read between the lines.

'You're still mad about that essay, aren't you?'

'It's just been a shitty sort of day all up. Can we do something?'

'I'll make some calls,' she promises. 'See if anything's going on.'

Grit my teeth when Terry gets home from work and Rose-Marie asks, on cue, her daily question about the weather forecast. *Any rain in sight?* The same four words every day, for weeks. I don't know how Terry hasn't strangled her. The mood I'm in, it takes all my will not to do it myself.

There isn't, but Rose-Marie doesn't give a damn about whether it rains or not. In fact, she'd probably prefer the drought lasts forever, so she doesn't have to deal with rain messing up her hair. She's just doing her bullshit dutiful wife thing. It makes me want to run away as fast as I can, and that's on a normal day. Today, if I have to deal with her shit much longer, I'm going to lose it.

But, even itching to get out of the house, I don't rush it. Scamming parents is about timing: hit them with all the information at once, and do it when they're distracted. I wait till Terry's pulling the defrosted meat out of the fridge, then: 'I'm not in for dinner tonight, remember.'

Terry puts the meat tray on the draining board. He raises an eyebrow, the cynic. He's harder to con than most of them. 'What are we supposed to remember?'

'Told you last week. Jem turned eighteen today so we're taking her out to dinner, just a group of us girls.'

'It's a Monday night.'

'I know, but it'll mean a heap to her. We won't be late. We're just going to Pancakes on the Rocks. Besides, I was home all Saturday night doing that essay, I'll go nuts if I don't get some time out. I've done all my homework.' The words roll off my tongue so easily. Too much practice.

I'm pretty sure he doesn't buy it, but he nods. 'Don't be late.'

I learned all about guns and cows and sheep from Peter White. He and Marianne had four boys of their own, and if Marianne was hoping that I would be the girl she'd always wanted she must have been sadly disappointed. In two weeks I could drive the sheep just as well as ten-year-old John. I lasted there for a year and a half, till I'd learned all there was to learn and discovered I was bored.

In six months with Sharna Appleby I learned about a) makeup and b) the tricks of the closet drinker. Jesse, my older foster brother, used to raid her secret supplies. Didn't take long to figure out what sort of places were good for hiding.

Learned how to play chess and how to never lose at noughts and crosses when I was six. With every new house, I learned new skills—how to barter in Spanish, how to make money on the stockmarket, how to drive a tractor and play the violin and pour the perfect beer. And none of them is as consistently useful as the art of telling people only what they want to hear. I was probably four or five when I discovered that people couldn't get mad at you if they never found out. If people want to call that manipulative, so be it. Far as I'm concerned, it's simple survival.

before
after
later

School becomes routine. The uniform becomes familiar. I guess I always knew it would, but it makes me sad somehow, too, as if now I've really left the old me, the old school and who I was behind.

Morgan is in the darkroom most days, and we chat. I tinker with photos, taking the time to ensure every negative is dust-free, every print perfect, because I'd rather be in there talking about Chagall and Picasso than sitting in the classroom listening to Sarah Bancroft recount the excesses of her social life.

I manage to get through till the last week of term one this way before Shepherd pins me down and demands to see what I have. I spread out my contact sheet and prints for her to see.

'What is it?'

'Architectural photography.'

She frowns, plays with the key necklace around her neck. 'The angles, sharpness of the image, the contrast… Technically, your images are perfect. But what's it *about*?'

'It's about how the manmade environment outlasts generations.'

'No.' She shakes her head. 'It's just not engaging me. What could you add to it? Do you do mixed media?' She reaches for my diary and starts flipping through the pages. I almost reach out to stop her, knowing what she'll find. Plenty of scribbles and sketches, vague mindmaps of stuff I could do that wouldn't involve too much time or emotional investment. All pretty shoddy, compared to what I used to do. I wouldn't be back at school if I wasn't prepared to put the effort in, do the mechanics of it, but at the end of the day I just want to get home. Go bush with Iago and try to avoid getting caught in another one-sided Mum argument. No more pouring heart and soul into an artwork or a drama piece. The things that used to seem so important to me just don't matter anymore.

'This is all your research? What about your work from last year, at your old school?'

'That's all in a separate diary.'

'I want to see it. Can you bring it next lesson?'

'I don't know where it is…' I hedge.

'Find it. I want to see what you're capable of.'

*

I take Iago down to the bush and I stretch out on my red gum and stare up at the sky. My art diary from last year is in a pile with all the rest of my art diaries, in the bottom of my wardrobe. I know exactly where it is because I haven't touched it for nearly a year.

My SLR is resting on my stomach, the strap wound around my wrist in case I lose my balance. The gum isn't much wider than me, and even though I'm here every other day I know it'll still only take one wrong move for me to end up in the knee-deep creek below. The SLR is a familiar weight, a familiar shape. Squat and square compared to the digitals, but it still takes kick-arse photos.

It's loaded up with black and white film. The bush is a bit overdone, really, if you look through my negatives collection. I shift precariously onto my stomach, point at the fresh growth wrapping itself around the rotting branches and snap away half-heartedly, knowing Shepherd will get mad if I've got nothing. I get a few shots off before Iago starts whining.

'All right, all right.' Time to keep moving.

We trudge up the hill. He knows the track as well as I do. He's surprisingly spry when he gets into the bush, launching himself over fallen branches and through the overgrowth like a puppy. Every few metres he stops and looks back, checking that I'm still coming, that I'm keeping up.

We get to the top and both take our time to catch

our breath. The sun is starting to go down and I know Mum'll be home soon and mad if she finds out where I am. Part of me instinctively guilts up at the thought of it, but it's in the back of my mind. I feel safe in the bush. I can't really believe in consequences, or any reality beyond trees and birds and Iago and me.

'What do you want to do?' I hear his voice, Robbie's voice, my doctor's voice, the school counsellor's voice. They all ask the same question. What do you want to do?

And my answer has never really changed, although it's got harder to believe. I want to change the world. I just don't know how anymore. And I'm afraid that it's going to demand too much of me.

I get home and a walk into the middle of a warzone. Mum's home early, and she's mad. She breaks off from whatever she's shouting at Alan and goes off at me in Italian.

'*Dove siete stati?*'

'Mum!' I cut her off. 'I'm fine. I had to get some photos for my major project, that's all.'

I could answer her in Italian, but I won't. Alan speaks enough phrases to make polite conversation with the rellies, but that's it. I feel rude having a conversation like that in front of him. It excludes him. And I'm annoyed at her because I know she does it deliberately. She was born here; she speaks English as well as anybody else. And she's doing it more and more since Robbie…

Mum storms out. She hates it when somebody interrupts her flow instead of just taking it. I love Alan but he needs to learn how to stand up to her.

I follow her into the kitchen.

'What did Alan do so wrong, anyway? Why do you have to pick on him all the time?'

'*Non è il vostro problema!*' She waves a spatula at me.

'Yeah, it is my problem! And speak English, Mum.'

'Your stepfather has no respect for my work!'

She always calls him that when she's annoyed. 'Your stepfather'. Typical irrational Mum. Alan has always been her biggest supporter and she knows it.

'What makes you think that?'

'He called my PA and cancelled a week's worth of my appointments. He has some crazy idea about going off to France. I have four clients scheduled that week.'

Somehow the more worked up she gets the calmer I stay. 'The holiday was my idea, Mum.'

'So now you're talking about me behind my back?'

It's not even worth arguing with her. 'Just stop getting so mad at Alan all the time. He's only trying to help.'

'Well, he doesn't know.'

'Doesn't know what?'

She stops, as if I've asked a question she's not willing to answer.

And a thought occurs to me, something so horrible yet simple that I don't know why I didn't think of it sooner. Is she putting the blame all on Alan simply so she doesn't have to blame me?

Our extension English teacher is starting to stress because we haven't covered everything in the syllabus and we're running out of time. I have ancient history and then legal and by lunch my hand is about to drop off, I've done so much writing. Anthony tells me to suck it up. He's just spent a double period in the hall while his drama teacher and the cast rehearse *King Lear*.

'They only have two weeks till opening night. Lordley was screaming at them, saying the whole thing was going to be a disaster.' He pauses, shrugs. 'He gets like that every year, though. It'll turn out okay. Morgan was there, she's actually pretty good.'

*

When I get home I nearly don't see Lauren on the couch. It's not somewhere I would ever think to look for her. She's the sort of person who thinks you're wasting time if you're not multitasking—that if you're going to be watching TV it'd better be something educational and you'd better be making yourself useful at the same time, like tidying the place up. But she's just sitting there, knees drawn up and not even a textbook in sight.

She looks up at me, draws her arms folded across her chest as if she's cold. There's something, a look, about her, that I don't know at all. Vulnerable; it gives me goosebumps. If she wants to talk about her feelings, I'm outta here.

'Where's Morgan?'

I stare at her, trying to make sense of her. 'She's got rehearsals at school till five.'

'How's she getting home?'

'She'll get a lift with someone.'

She nods, looks around the room as if she can't handle making eye contact. Tells the coffee table: 'Dad's back.'

'What?' I've misheard her, I'm sure.

'He's in Sydney. Got a job at one of the big firms in the city.'

'How do you know?'

'One of my lecturers knows him, they used to work together.' She adds, 'He's got a new wife and a kid.'

I take the news the way it was delivered: quietly.

Without a word I drop down onto the other couch, surprised. I don't feel upset, I don't want to get angry. I don't feel anything, really.

I used to wonder, from time to time, what sort of new life he would build for himself. After a few years, when the airmailed presents and letters had long ceased arriving, I began to forget that we had ever had a father. I haven't thought about him in years. I can't even remember his face. Does that make me a terrible son, or him a terrible father?

'Does Mum know?' I ask finally.

'I doubt it.'

'Should we tell Morgan?'

A shrug. 'What would be the point?'

'Maybe she'd want to see him.'

Morgan was three when he left. If I can't remember his face, what chance does she have? And does that make her more or less likely to want to see him?

I look at Lauren. If she doesn't want to tell Morgan, why is she telling me?

'Would you go see him?'

'I don't know.'

'You hated him.' I can remember that much—her screaming it, not caring who heard. Making all sorts of threats about what she'd do to him if she ever saw him again. Typical Lauren.

'I didn't hate him.'

'You burned effigies of him on the barbeque.'

105

'So I was mad at him for leaving. I didn't hate him.'

'Try telling that to Morgan's Ken dolls.'

The ghost of an ironic smile. She looks at me, still with that sad, tired expression, like after all these years she's realised she doesn't have all the answers; doesn't really know anything at all.

'What's uni like?'

She's midway through her second year, but it's a question I haven't dared asked before.

'Just...' She stares hard at the floor for a moment, then pushes herself up off the couch. 'Don't grow up too fast. It's not all as easy as it looks.'

Morgan doesn't get home till nearly nine and Lauren gets mad.

'I thought your rehearsal finished at five.'

'We went over.'

'You stink of cigarette smoke.'

'Shut up.'

I follow Morgan into her room. She kicks off her shoes, tosses her bag to the floor and then kicks it again for good measure. The floor is a mess of dirty clothes, school books, CDs, art supplies. She painted a purple feature wall last year; now it's covered with photos and pencil scribbling—song lyrics, quotes from artists, little cartoony characters she's created. There's a clay sculpture on her desk, a gargoyle-like thing with eyes and limbs everywhere. I pick it up carefully. Weigh it in my hands as I try to figure out what to say. I've never been a big brother to Morgan. Even when Lauren took off, I didn't take over being the boss, I just figured Morgan and I were old enough to do our own thing. Maybe I should have.

'This is hideous.'

'You don't think there can be beauty in ugliness?' she asks defiantly.

I smile slightly at her earnestness. 'Don't worry about Lauren. She's just in a mood.'

'She hasn't changed. She thinks she has the right to come back and tell us what to do.'

'Actually...' I hesitate; if Lauren's relentless bullying over the years taught me anything it's that it's not a good idea to even have an opinion, let alone voice it. I push myself. 'I think she has.'

'Yeah?' Morgan's annoyed with me too, now. 'She's still being a total bitch to me.'

Even as I try to find the words to explain what I've seen, I know Morgan's not going to listen. She's too wrapped up in her own perspective to see it. Empathy has never been her thing.

I move a little bit closer, watching as she starts picking up dirty clothes. She does smell like cigarette smoke. Not just her clothes, but her breath, too. I'm close enough to smell it. And something else—beer, maybe?

'You know smoking's a really hard habit to break, right?'

She gives me a look. 'I don't smoke.'

'Morgs…Just don't get started, okay?'

'Fine. Whatever.' She turns away from me, and I know I've blown my chance. I don't even know if I was going to tell her about Dad or not.

I'm on the driveway doing some quick warm-up stretches when I hear a shout. 'Hey, McAlpine!'

Kayla. She sits on the rails of her front porch sometimes to smoke and watch the world go by. I've never quite worked out why; maybe it's part of her image. Most kids at school can be slotted into one box or another easily enough, but she's one of the few that defy definition. Sometimes it seems like she's trying to be punk or goth: eyebrow piercing, drooping cigarette; long, kind-of-creepy stares. But she's in the top maths class and she does extension English with me, and if somebody says something she disagrees with she'll practically jump on them. Beat them to death with a scary intensity and an even scarier vocab. She got in trouble last week for calling the head teacher of English an 'obtuse narcissist whose greatest mistake is thinking that verbosity is a sign of erudition'. She's the sort of person, to be honest, I wouldn't ever want to meet in a dark alley. I've known her more than half my life and she still makes me nervous.

I wouldn't let her know that, of course.

I eye the cigarette dangled between her index and middle fingers, trying to act casual. 'You know, nicotine is ten times more addictive than heroin.'

She grins. 'Who says this is nicotine?'

She likes pushing people's buttons. I know that. I see it every day in English. So I don't give her the satisfaction of reacting. I just turn and take off. I don't get far, though, before I hear pounding footsteps behind me, somebody trying to catch up. 'Hey, hold up.'

She's now empty-handed, untied laces on her Converse hightops whipping as she runs. She draws alongside, out of breath from the sprint. 'Hey, McAlpine, I said slow down!' Annoyed.

'If you had full lung capacity you'd be able to keep up with me,' I say with a shrug, picking up my pace to sprint to the end of the street.

Another thing I know about Kayla—she's competitive. When we were kids the three of us used to go over to her place to play. She'd treat each game of Connect Four or Hide and Seek as if it was an Olympic final, and she was always, always, determined to win. Any time she and Lauren went head-to-head on something you were pretty much guaranteed fireworks. Lauren was older, but they were both scary smart, and Kayla wasn't above using her fists when she ran out of words. She still isn't. These days it just takes her longer to run out of words.

'I just—wanna—ask—you a—question.' She pushes just ahead, so I have to accelerate to catch up. I feel the burn in my chest.

'What?'

'Chaucer.'

I don't know if she's yanking my chain or what. But she's tiring and I want to rub it in. 'Meet you at the end of the street,' and I take off.

It's a fifty-metre sprint, both of us feet-slapping, breaths coming short and sharp. I can feel her right behind me. My mouth is dry and my chest feels like it's about to explode but I've got some of that McAlpine stubborn streak too, and I'm not going to let her win. I hurl myself forwards, crossing an invisible finish line the winner. She stumbles in behind me.

A second to catch my breath. Pacing. 'See?' I manage, hands behind my head.

'Yeah, you were always faster than me.'

I might not be great at sports—mostly because I just don't really care about kicking a ball into a net or tossing it through a hoop—but one thing I can do is run. Being in that zone, where your heart is racing and your pulse is deafening, is like being in another world. It's the next best thing after reading.

We walk for the next hundred metres or so, silent while we get our breath back.

'What makes you think I understand Chaucer any better than you do?' We've just started studying *The Canterbury Tales* and you can tell the whole class is bewildered.

'You're a book nerd. I figured if anybody understands it, it'd be you.'

A spark of annoyance. I know what people think of me, but you'd think if she's asking for my help she could at least refrain from insulting me for five minutes. 'Book nerd?'

She gives me a blasé shrug. 'Ninety percent of the time I see you, you've got a book in your hands. I'm not judging, I'm just saying that's the world you live in, you speak the language. And I need a translator...'

Suddenly I'm over it. If I want to be insulted and demeaned by a girl, I have sisters for that. 'Race you back.'

I get the lead on her this time but it's still a battle. We both skid to a finish on my driveway, but I don't really care who wins. I mutter something about water and take off into the house without looking back.

The house is quiet. Half past ten and Mum's presumably upstairs, Lauren and Morgan in their bedrooms. I stand in the middle of the living room and look around, suddenly feeling a sort of hopeless claustrophobia. Feeling like if I don't make myself step out, I'll stay hiding here, and I'll end up like my mother and everything I pity about her.

before
after
later

Morning hits. The blast of the alarm, the foul taste in my mouth, the too-much light in the room.

Shit.

I'm still in my skinny jeans and top from last night; peel them off in the bathroom, leaving red seams on my skin. Grass, both kinds, falls out of the folds of my clothes onto the tiles. A string of tired, hungover expletives. My stomach starts to knot itself up, and I scrub at my skin in the shower till it goes red raw. My head is killing me.

Rose-Marie is alone in the kitchen, sitting at the table with her coffee and newspaper. Tash is nowhere to be seen. Terry's keys are gone from the hook. Rose-Marie looks up. My heart starts to hammer in my chest.

'He had an early meeting,' she explains coldly. 'He's dropping her off on his way.'

Feels like I should launch into an apology, or an excuse, but it's only going to get me into more trouble. I don't remember anything after about nine last night. Went to The Gap and sat in the back of Tim's van with a whole lot of beer and dope, weed with an ocean view. Don't even remember getting home. Been years since I lost it that badly. And I feel like shit.

She stands up. 'Anything you want to say?'

She's never really got mad at me before. Frustrated, sure, when I have to be asked three times to set the table or change a nappy. But she's really angry. Didn't she do this sort of thing when she was younger? Ha. Dumb question. Terry might have. Private school boy with Daddy's money to burn, I reckon he was the sort. Not Rose-Marie.

'Sorry I was late. I lost track of time...'

'You were off your face.'

'I didn't—'

'Do you even remember talking to Terry last night? He thought somebody was breaking in and it was you, so drunk you couldn't get your key in the lock.'

Okay, change of tactics. 'Look, it was a mistake, okay? I got a bad mark for an essay and it really shook me up. I had a few drinks. Don't tell me you've never done that.'

'How long have you been doing drugs?'

'What?'

'We're not stupid, Eliat. Terry says you were reeking of marijuana.'

Don't answer that. Don't give her anything.

'Terry and I are going to have to talk about what to do. Obviously we've been letting you have too much independence and not enough responsibility around here. It's time for you to start pulling your weight a bit more.' She sighs. 'Terry and I accept some of the blame for this. We should have known.'

It's designed to sting, and it does. Somehow I'm not really surprised by the sudden vindictiveness of it. For all her talk about clean slates and fresh starts, there's a sort of satisfaction in her words now. She's been waiting two years to say them.

Long day. Extension two maths at lunch and by the end of the day my brain is useless. All the teachers have piled on homework and I manage to plod through half of it while Tash rides her tricycle in tight circles in the backyard. I know which teachers will check and which ones won't, but don't want to give Terry and Rose-Marie anything else to bitch about, so I even do my chem work. God, school work is boring.

Sentencing takes place after dinner: Eliat Singleton's social life is suspended until further notice. To start:

grounded for the next week, including the weekend. No going out with friends, absolutely no parties. That sounds bad enough, but then something else hits me. 'It's school holidays!'

'Then you'll have plenty of time to study,' says Rose-Marie coldly.

Terry's quiet, doesn't even look at me. Soon as the laws are laid down he mutters something about making sure Tash is asleep, and bolts. I thought he'd be above giving me the silent treatment.

It feels like I have to say something to defend myself, try to worm my way out somehow. 'It was one time.'

Rose-Marie stares at me. Her face is asking if I actually expect her to take my word for that.

I never had trouble getting myself moved from one place to the next. Always easy enough to please people, be who they wanted me to be. When I got fed up, I just stopped trying. Learned quickly enough nobody wanted a kid around who bit or bullied or talked back. Never anything bad enough to get myself in real trouble, I just made myself impossible. Unlikeable. Keep that up long enough and they'll find a reason not to have room for you anymore.

In my bedroom I sit and stare at the carpet. Telling myself it's strategic, I'm paving the way for an exit. Wishing I believed it.

before
after
later

This time I beat him to the cafe. As I wait I wonder if he'll think I was silly to call him.

'I'm sorry.'

Dropping into his seat, he raises an eyebrow. 'For what?'

'I don't know. It's just kinda weird, me calling you.'

'If it makes you feel less awkward, you can think of yourself as the high-maintenance little sister I never had.'

I'll wear that. 'Okay.'

'So what's up, kid?'

'It's stupid.' Not what I'm thinking about, or even the fact that I want to tell someone, but that he's the one I want to tell.

'I've done stupid. Not much in the realms of stupid that can surprise me.'

'I'm worried about my parents.'

'Worried like it's-going-to-end-in-divorce?'

'Maybe. They used to fight sometimes, but now it's basically every night. Mum's being awful and Alan just takes it.'

'What are they fighting about?'

'I don't even know. Stupid stuff, from the sounds of it. No matter what he does it's the wrong thing. It just feels like things are starting to disintegrate and it's unfair. We already lost Robbie...'

'A few fights doesn't mean the end of things. Stuff like this takes a while to get over.'

'Yeah, but...' I trail off as the waitress approaches, not quite sure what I was going to say, anyway. I keep thinking back to the last thing Mum said in the argument, about Alan not knowing. Not knowing what?

I deliberately keep the conversation on lighter topics. He tells me about his work, about travelling. I've heard some of it before. I remember him talking to me that night in the pouring rain, trying to distract me by telling me stuff, stories about people and places. He's just spent two months volunteering in Africa, in the Congo. He's planning on going back for a longer stint, a couple of years, maybe.

'You're not worried about being away for so long?'

'I don't know,' he says with a shrug. He braces

himself against the table again in that characteristic way. He's the same person as before, but different, too. Last time there was something about him, some sadness that went beyond the situation we were in. Whatever had caused it, it seems to be gone now. 'I look at myself and wonder if I'm running away. But maybe that's exactly where I'm meant to be.'

'You're still thinking about them, aren't you?' he asks as we stand to leave.

'How can I not? If you think about it, it's all my fault.'

'Are you serious?'

'If I hadn't crashed and Robbie hadn't died, Mum would have nothing to get angry about. It'd all be fine, like it was before.' I'm not saying it to make him feel sorry for me, I'm just stating the facts.

He grabs my arm, but then releases it almost immediately, as if he's conscious of overstepping some boundary. 'Can you hear yourself? Are you seriously trying to tell me you think you're to blame for what happened? I was there, I saw it happen. None of this is your fault. Least of all your mum's issues. You were just in the wrong place at the wrong time.'

All that stuff is true, but he's still wrong. Yeah, the other driver made mistakes too, but that doesn't let me off. I'm still the reason we were sitting at that exact intersection at that exact moment. Wrong place and wrong time, exactly.

*

Alan's out when I get home. Tuesday nights he plays indoor cricket. Mum's sitting at the kitchen bench with dirty dishes piled up around her and a stack of design magazines in front, flipping through and flagging pages. Tear sheets, they're called. She's got folders and pinboards full of the things at work and in her office here.

I've never been into domestic stuff but I'm probably better at it than Mum. She doesn't even know how to use the dishwasher. I start rinsing the dirty dishes and loading them in.

'Why are you so mad at Alan?'

'*Dio!*' She throws up her hands. 'Can't I just have a moment's peace?'

'I just asked you a simple question.'

She glares at me, then starts flipping pages again with renewed violence. 'I'm not discussing this with you.'

'You said he doesn't know. What is it that he doesn't know? Is this about Robbie?' Surely it must be—what else would it be? But what about Robbie?

'He wants us to move on. Go on holidays. Act that it's all normal.'

'What's so wrong with that? What else are we supposed to do?' I want to move on. I need the wound to close up and stop hurting so much.

'It's been less than a year since we put your brother in the ground. Fifteen years of life and we can't take twelve months to remember him? But your stepfather,

119

no, he doesn't want to *waste* the time…'

'Mum!'

'How can he know? How can he know a mother's pain? To lose Robbie, to almost lose you…' She's unstoppable once she gets momentum. 'Your stepfather wants this to be like one of his cases, that he can tie up all the loose ends and pack it away in a box and move on. If he really knew the pain—'

'Mum, shut up!' It's the only thing I can say. 'Stop talking like you're the only one who got hurt.' Even as the words come out of my mouth I realise: that's how she actually feels. She thinks that Alan, because he's not our biological father, doesn't feel the grief as strongly as she does. It's stupid. And typical of Mum, egocentric, emotional Mum, to think that way. Yeah, it changed her life. But it changed my life and Alan's too. And Daniel's. Any one of those other people who were there helping or watching could have been affected too and we'll never know. Has she ever stopped to think about that? Probably not.

Once her business took off she started working longer hours. It was Alan who took me and Robbie to soccer training and our games on weekends, who took us swimming and helped us with our homework. I don't remember a time before he came on the scene. One of my earliest memories is being in the backyard of our old house with him, and he was spinning me around till we both got dizzy. I was only four or five, Robbie two years younger. That was when they were dating, and soon after that they got married and every morning he'd put on a full spread for breakfast; not just cereal but porridge and fruit and pancakes. We thought it was the best thing ever. He still makes the best breakfasts.

'I always thought of him as my dad,' I say finally. 'So did Robbie. Don't take that away from us.'

On that note, I leave her. My bedroom is dark and I flip on the light and gaze around. My eyes fall on the pile of canvases, and before I can second-guess myself I pick up the top one and take it over to my workbench, ripping off the plastic wrapping. I choose my tin of red paint and crack it open. It's started to separate, too long since it was last used, and I have to grab a brush and stir and stir until it thickens again.

I paint a line, a delicate curve. The edge of a leaf, the curve of a woman's buttock, I don't know. I reach for blue and repeat the move on the inside of the curve, a thinner line, then I grab a half-empty glass of water from beside my bed and dump the contents into my painting mug, wash the brush until the water is brilliant blue. I bring the blue back to the canvas and water down the second line, then with the wash I round out the shape. An orchid petal? I dab off the excess water so only a thin shadow is left, then swap brushes again and open the white, laying on a thick coat, then scratching back. Orchid petal. Tame. Somewhere to start.

I paint another petal, then do the quick outline of

the lip and the three narrower petals at the back, then I fill the background with a rusty orange wash. Average. It needs something. I look around my room; something to inspire me, even something to collage with. My photo wall. People, places, random textures and colours. Tanned feet in bright pink Havaianas. Sunburnt grass. Monkey bars. Fingernails painted with the Australian flag. Lime green stick insects with bulging black eyes. I used to be a scavenger with the camera, not interested so much in faces but in little details. A childlike collection of postcards from the world around me. And that's the problem with it. I'm not a child anymore.

I leave the canvas behind and move closer to the wall, stretch hesitantly up. I can't even reach the highest row of photos. Instead of pulling down the lower ones I stop and get a chair. But again, I can't bring myself to tear them down. These photos came with me, in their embryonic form, from our old house six years ago. Every night I've gone to bed staring at them and woken up the same way, reminded of Robbie every time. Pulling them down is a big deal.

The digital camcorder is still in its original box in my wardrobe. We got it right before the crash. I think Mum and Alan just forgot about it.

I flip it to playback to check I'm not going to record over anything, but the tape's blank. I grab my tripod and set up the camcorder so my whole room is in frame— wall, workbench, unmade bed—and I hit record.

It's going to be like pulling off a bandaid, I know. I climb up onto my chair so I can reach the top corner and I pull. The photos are stuck to the wall, not each other, and only the photo in my hand comes off. Not good enough. Not fast enough. I'll lose courage at this rate.

I grab off another picture, then another, and start clawing at them, shoving my hands underneath trying to prise them free. They start to fall to the ground around me, but still not good enough. I start to tear the photos, throwing them over my shoulder. Grabbing them with both hands and crushing the prints in my hands. Trashing my wall, wanting to feel some sort of breakthrough or release, wanting to want to bawl my eyes out. But it just all feels mechanical, that brief sense of flight that came with painting is gone. I pull the last photo off and survey the mess on the floor, and then the blobs of Blu-Tack all over the wall, and I just feel empty.

It takes twice as long to pull off all the Blu-Tack as it did to get the photos off, and it leaves greasy marks on the paint. Too bad. Mum can just redo this room like she's been itching to for years.

I gather up all the trashed photos, trying not to look at them, and shove them in a shopping bag to put out in the garbage later. And I stare at the wall. Empty. I flip off the bedroom light, but the moonlight coming

123

through the window hits the bare wall, emphasising its barrenness.

The camcorder is still recording a failed experiment. I take it off the tripod, flip it to playback mode and hit rewind, listening to it zoom back to the start of the tape as I carry it back to my bed to watch.

Robbie. The voice, tinny because of the tiny camcorder but still unmistakeably his, fills my ears, the room. April last year, the digital readout tells me.

'Hey, I got it working. It's recording me, genius tech guy.' He swings the camera around, panning over the same photo montage I just pulled down. He's in my bedroom. We must have unpacked it in here. He lands the camera on me. I'm on my bed in my pyjamas, cross-legged with my art diary in my lap, scribbling madly away. Same sheets, doona; even the same pyjamas. How can that be?

'Sarah, say hi.'

On the tiny screen, Old-me holds up a hand, ignoring him. 'Go away.'

'Stop being such a wuss. Say hi.'

Old-me looks at the camera. A sardonic smile. 'Hi. Happy now?'

'Is that the way you talk to guys? No wonder you can't get a date.' He swings the camera back on himself, giving himself a smug thumbs-up for the crack. He was going through the hair product stage, and his hair is cut short and carefully spiked up. His face goes serious, newsreader style.

'Robert Starke reporting, National Nine News.'

And that's it. It cuts to me, my bedroom, and the wall that is no more. I hit the stop button and lean back on my pillows, holding the camcorder against my chest as if it can somehow ease the fresh pain there. I thought tearing down the wall would end something; move me on. But seeing his face and hearing his voice has brought him back in such an intense way. I can barely breathe. Not what I wanted. Not fair.

Part of me wants to erase the tape or just destroy the whole thing, but I know I could never bring myself to do it. I can't put it down, either. Without moving it from my chest I nudge the power to Off with my thumb, and I lie there silently in the dark holding it, trying not to cry.

Lauren finds me sitting on the front sandstone step reading Chaucer, or at least trying to. My mind is swimming with too much else to concentrate properly. Anthony spent last period trying to talk me into his new plan for schoolies, a week on the Gold Coast with a bunch of guys from our grade. I tuned him out as soon as he started talking about hot girls in bikinis. I know for a fact the closest he's ever got to a girl in a bikini is when he had to be fished out of a rip last summer by a female lifeguard.

Lauren never went to schoolies. It's a tradition she views with scorn, like she does any sort of organised social event. To her, anything less than a stubborn refusal to participate in a social activity is a betrayal of one's right to independent thought. She took off to Papua New Guinea for two months instead, using money she'd saved up at her after-school job.

'Don't you have homework?'

'This is my homework.'

Realising that line of attack has no legs at all, she looks me up and down. Notices my jeans. 'Seriously?'

I know straight away what she's talking about, but I feign ignorance, just because it's one of the few weapons I have. 'What?'

'Are you wearing designer jeans?'

From her voice you'd think I was wearing something made of puppy fur. Yeah, I'm wearing Diesel jeans. Morgan, in one of her generous moods, announced a few months ago that she was taking me clothes shopping, because 'it's the only chance you have of ever getting a girlfriend'.

I'm not so stubbornly set on being an outsider that I was going to turn her down. I don't really care what I wear, but if looking like I belong is going to make my life easier, why not? Even Morgan was pretty happy with the end result.

An exasperated noise from Lauren, a sort of frustrated sigh. 'Why do you have to do that?'

'What?'

'Act like everybody else. Follow the herd.'

'Be normal, you mean? What's so wrong with being ordinary?'

'Ordinary people don't change the world.'

'But what if I don't want to change the world? What if I just want to live a normal life and just be happy and try to make the people around me happy? Why is that so wrong?'

'Because it's lazy and selfish.'

'I wear designer jeans and that makes me lazy or selfish? Why do you waste all your energy on making such a big deal out of stuff that doesn't even matter?'

Normally a comment I would keep to myself, it slips out before I can think. Lauren stares at me. Surprised, I think, that I've argued back. I push away the feeling. Of course I want the world to be a better place. Doesn't everybody? That's why people give money to drought-stricken countries and malnourished orphans. But life here goes on, too.

'Look at the world! People have just sat back and done shit-all for too long. People like you who just sit back and think other people are going to solve all the problems. So we've got global warming and terrorists blowing people up and still people don't really care, unless it happens to *them*, or their families or people they love…It's just shit.'

It's a standard Lauren rant. Sometimes I think she doesn't even know what she's trying to say, she just needs to say something, to vent her frustrations at a world she can't fix.

She leans against the side of the house, as if the

tirade has worn her out. More quietly. 'Only a quarter of HIV-positive people in Zimbabwe have access to anti-retrovirals. That's three thousand Zimbabweans dying unnecessarily every week. Tuberculosis kills about two million people a year worldwide. Malnutrition kills five million children…that's thirty thousand a day. What are we going to do about it?'

We? Since when was this stuff I had to worry about? I have English essays and history assignments and hours' worth of homework to do. I have exams coming up and schoolies to get out of.

'It's not up to us to solve all the world's problems,' I say, defending myself. 'We can't do everything.'

'Yeah, well, we should at least be doing something.'

She disappears into the house. I try to get back to Chaucer but it's too difficult to concentrate, so I head into my bedroom to work on my maths homework. Morgan arrives home about half an hour later; I can hear her banging around in the kitchen. I find her tipping raw pasta into a microwaveable container. When Morgan's upset, she cooks.

'What happened?'

'I'm mad.'

'About what?'

'Everything.' She slams the fridge door shut, explodes. 'You haven't even got tickets.'

'What?'

'Exactly.'

Tickets...I've got so stuck inside my own head it takes me a second to realise what she's talking about. Her play. They've been selling them at school, and I keep thinking I should buy one and not knowing if Lauren would come watch it. If we could get Mum out of the house to come too. Delaying, really, because I think I know what the answer from both of them will be, and I don't want to have to face it, for Morgan's sake.

'I never said I wasn't coming, I just haven't got one yet. I was going to see if Lauren and Mum were coming.'

'I don't want them there.' She shoves the pasta container under the tap and twists the water on violently. It hits the pasta and sprays back out in all directions. She swears.

I'm not brave—or stupid—enough to offer to help. Instead, I slide onto a bar stool and pick up the mail someone's tossed down on the granite countertop. A water bill for Mum, a bank statement for Lauren and—

'What's this?'

Torn scraps of paper and envelope. I turn one piece over and there's handwriting on the back. The tight scrawl immediately makes my stomach drop. Dad's. I didn't think I'd even recognise it after all this time.

I turn the pieces over one by one, carefully sliding them into position like jigsaw puzzle pieces, until I have two complete A4 pages in front of me. I can hear Morgan sorting violently through the cutlery drawer but my eyes are stuck to the page, skimming the words. It's an apology and explanation and entreaty all in one. I wonder if it was Morgan who tore it up, or Lauren. I can picture Lauren tearing up the envelope the moment she recognised the writing, without even glancing over its contents. Leaving it out on display just to prove that she doesn't give a damn.

'How come you didn't tell me?'

When I finally look up, I find Morgan standing there with hands on her hips and angry tears in her eyes. She still grips, absurdly, a spatula in her left hand, resting it against her leg.

Morgan was always the tantrum thrower. I don't remember ever throwing a tantrum. I can't even remember the last time I cried, the last time I actually felt anything passionately enough.

'We only found out last week.'

'Have you seen him?'

'No.'

'Were you going to tell me?'

I don't know the answer to that question. I get the feeling no matter what answer I give her she'll be upset. I slide down off the bar stool and hold out my hands, wanting to make peace, somehow. 'Morgs…'

Not interested. She pushes past me, not to her bedroom but towards the front door, scooping up her shoes as she goes. She's still in school uniform, but that doesn't seem to be holding her back.

*

It's nearly eleven when I hear her arrive back home. A car drops her off, some P-plater with a giant muffler, from the sounds of it. A few minutes later I hear her in the bathroom, throwing up.

Maybe it's not the whole world we need to save. Maybe we should be starting one person at a time.

before
after
later

It was Jonah Morris who taught me how to jam up the public phones. Three o'clock in the morning walking from his place to mine, and we had to stop twice for him to take a piss against a gum tree.

'C'mere, Ellie.' Pulled me against him. His mouth was hot and tasted of beer as he kissed me, tongue as clumsy as his legs. I pushed him off.

'Your fly's still undone.'

'Nobody's looking.'

Nobody around to look. Too late and too early for the truckies heading up the highway, or even Mrs McCormack, who'd take her Alzheimer's for an early morning walk and not be able to find her way home. Just the two of us, on the road, two k's from Brian and Shirl's rundown place on the hill.

Servo up ahead of us. Dark and deserted, with a street-light in front that lit up the public phone. Jonah grabbed my hand—his was sticky (with what, I didn't want to know) and tugged.

'C'mon. Show you something.'

He put the beer bottle down rather than let go my hand. Propped it on the edge of the shelf that held the phonebooks: watched the beer slosh in the bottle, back and forth, only a gulp or two left. Jonah wouldn't drink it anyway. Always tastes like shit, he said, and started working the keypad. Hit the right numbers enough times and…there you go. Out of service. For the third time this month. I hadn't known it was Jonah; wasn't surprised, though. Sort of idiotic thing he'd think was hilarious.

'I am awesome.'

'You're a dickhead.'

Didn't even flinch, just grinned. God I was sick of that place, of Brian and Shirl, even Jonah. Two months in that stinking hole in the middle of nowhere.

I tugged the hand holding mine, not trying to get away but pulling him. Hating him in a way, but wanting to lose myself whatever it took. 'Let's go.'

'Where?'

'Somewhere dark.' He had a whole other set of tricks to get up to in the dark.

I learned lots of things from Jonah, but nothing that would get me anywhere except in trouble.

*

'Hold on…' I slap the groping hands off me. 'I can't.'

'You can't what?'

'Can't do this. Have to go.'

'Go where?'

'Home.'

I can't even remember this guy's name. Scott? He drops his hands to my hips and starts to work them upwards under my top as he kisses me. He tastes like beer, like Jonah Morris. After a while, they all taste like Jonah. I pull away from him again, more determined this time, though I know I'm losing the battle. Why is it always so much easier to just let them?

'I'm serious. I have to go.'

'Ten minutes.'

Nearly nine. It'll take at least thirty minutes for me to get home. Depends on whether the buses are running on time. I could stay another five…

The thought of having to face Terry and Rose-Marie decides it for me. My first time out of the house in a week, and I won't hear the end of it if I stuff up. Pull away, half regretful, half indifferent.

'Sorry. Next time.'

Tash is snoring. Blocked nose. Flat on her back, covers kicked off, breathing noisily through her mouth. She has a dozen pairs of pyjamas she loves to wear but when she overheats they end up all over the room and she sleeps in just her nappy.

135

Drop a kiss on her forehead. Feels warm and sweaty. A cold starting, or just the warm night? Nearly the end of April and we're still jetting these summery nights. I'm sure Terry has some boring explanation why.

'Eliat.' Rose-Marie standing at the top of the stairs in her DJs silk pyjamas. She's obviously been waiting up for me. Hair and makeup still faultless. She doesn't even have to think about being perfect. From her impeccably manicured nails to the way she sets the dinner table, it's just how she is. God, I hate her.

'Lounge room.' She gestures downstairs.

Terry is already in there. Ten minutes late and I'm up for night court.

They sit together on the leather lounge, the framed Ken Duncan on the wall behind. Rose-Marie has tidied Tash's drawing table and put all her toys away in their boxes.

'Did you forget that we set a curfew? Because I don't know how you could possibly forget, when that's the last thing we said before you went out the door. Did you even do any school work?'

'We got a whole chapter summary done. But then it ended up a big D&M...April's having issues with her parents.' April is my acceptable friend, moderate enough for Terry and Rose-Marie. She's always a good excuse. They've never met Izzy. As far as I'm concerned they never will.

'D&M?' Rose-Marie echoes dubiously.

Seriously? 'Deep and Meaningful.' Still blank looks. 'Serious discussion. Peer counselling. That thing friends do.' Feel like I'm just digging myself in deeper, but they won't buy it without the details.

Terry speaks. He's barely spoken to me over the last week. Forget the easy banter, I've been lucky to get eye contact. 'The first night, Eliat, and you've already blown it. What do you expect us to do?'

'I'm only ten minutes late! And what was I supposed to do, just leave her there crying?'

'Yes!' He looks frustrated, fed up with my shit. 'You had a chance and you blew it,' he repeats. 'You're officially grounded for the rest of the holidays. And don't even bother trying to talk your way out of it. I'm not interested in any more of your stories.'

'Fine.' Everything inside me is busting to have this fight but I learned a long time ago that arguing is the least effective way of getting what I want. 'Can I go now?'

Attic bedroom. Peel off my clothes. They still smell faintly of cigarette smoke, despite the perfume and deodorant. Open my window wide and hang them off the window frame, letting them dangle in the breeze.

Neat stack of freshly folded washing on the end of my bed. Rose-Marie's work. Pick it up to put on my desk to deal with later. Stop. Bunch of brochures on my desk that I didn't put there. Local private schools.

That sick feeling stirs up in the bottom of my stomach again. Still don't know why. After a moment's hesitation, drop the pile of washing right on top. Blot the whole thing from my mind.

Tash. Go see Tash.

Still sound asleep, face set. Something in that face tells you she's a tough little bugger, even while she's sleeping. She was stubborn at dinner, didn't want to eat her peas. Feels like days ago now.

Sit on the edge of her bed, watch the rise and fall of her chest. Fists are still clenched, as if she's re-fighting the pea battle in her dreams. The heaviness, the responsibility, starts to settle over me.

Stand. Shake it off.

Three years till Tash starts school. Let Rose-Marie make her plans, if it makes her feel good. Doesn't mean we have to stick to them, doesn't mean we even have to be around in three years. Or next year, or even next month.

'What do you reckon, kiddo?' I whisper. 'Have a think about it. We can do whatever you want. You just let me know.'

Think of Jesse O'Sullivan, and that look he'd get in his eyes when the pot kicked in and he started to talk. *Nobody owns me,* he'd repeat. *Nobody owns me.* I used to think that was me too. Except when he said it, it was like he was reminding, promising himself. *Nobody owns me.*

Nobody owned me either, but it was different. Didn't have to convince myself of it. The way I grew up there was nothing else. House to house, family to family, school to school. Only thing that stayed consistent was me. Nobody owned me. Unlike Jesse, that made me free.

before
after
later

Friday morning and I can't get out of bed. I lie there, hand still through the camcorder strap. It's a solid little piece of technology: I accidentally rolled over and slept on it and it still looks fine. My ribs are sore, though.

I don't want to watch the video again but I don't want to forget about it, either. When Mum comes in to wake me up, I hide it under my pillow and mumble something about a sore throat.

Alan comes in ten minutes later. 'Are you really sick or do you just need a day off school?'

'You really want to know?'

'Well, if you're sick I won't offer to make you blueberry pancakes…'

He makes me smile. 'Is Mum gone yet?'

'She'll be out the door in two minutes.'

On cue, Mum shouts a goodbye up the stairs followed by a string of unintelligible instructions. I must make a face, because Alan smiles. 'A bit like that, huh?'

As he moves towards the door I pull out the camcorder from under my pillow. 'Can I show you something?'

He comes back and sits on the end of the bed, waiting for the tape to rewind. I hand it to him in silence, because what would I say? It starts to play and I feel my stomach tumble. Robbie's voice. I draw my knees up and hug them. Watch Alan watching it. He's got a good poker face, but I can see his jaw tighten just the tiniest bit.

It reaches the end and he carefully closes the display screen. 'Where was this?'

'In my wardrobe. I forgot he filmed it...'

Neither of us is naive enough to think about getting Mum to watch it. But some day we might want to use the camcorder and we can't just tape over it.

Alan hands the camcorder back. 'You can copy this to your computer, can't you? Burn it to a DVD?'

'Yeah.'

'That's a start, then.' He stands. 'You go have a shower, I'll get started on your pancakes.'

We sit at the kitchen table. One of Mum's favourite pieces: solid antique mahogany...maybe teak. I tend to zone out when she goes on. I do know it was made in

141

nineteenth-century France. That's the one thing I love about it. A lot of people have sat around this table over the years.

Alan dishes up the pancakes for me and one for himself, then pours us both juice. He seems serious, more so than usual. 'You need to know that Mum and I have been talking.'

A chill down my spine. I hate conversations that start like this. I dig into the pancakes as if I don't know what's coming.

'You need to know...' He always starts off that way when he has to break bad news. 'That I don't want to leave you, or this house, or your mother. But we've talked about it and we're thinking it might do us both some good to have a break.'

'Talked about it? You mean Mum went off, as usual. Stop making excuses for her!' I probably sound annoyed at him, but it's Mum, really. What a stupid idea. She's buried so deep in her own self-pity she thinks this will make it better? Really?

'That's the stupidest thing I ever heard! She's so full of crap.'

'This comes from me too, Sarah.'

I stare at him, try to read his face. 'You said you don't want to leave.'

'And I don't. But if things keep going at this rate, we might get to the point where I do.'

'That doesn't make any sense.'

'I love your mother. But I can only take so much of this, and she won't let me help her. So either I step back now and give her the time to work through it herself, or we get to the point where we can't stand each other and I really do choose to walk away.'

'You'd never do that.'

He shrugs. 'You tell me. Am I supposed to just keep being her punching bag?'

'No! Stand up to her. Tell her to stop being so sorry for herself.'

'You really want me to pull the pin out of that grenade?'

His answer sucks. But at the same time he's totally right. That's probably what sucks about it. I push the plate of pancakes away. 'It's not fair.'

'I know it's not.'

I look around the kitchen, half expecting to see bags of his stuff piled up, but nothing looks any different.

'So are you moving out, or what?'

'Not yet. Nothing's decided yet. I just wanted to give you a heads-up…let you know what might be coming.'

I think back to how they used to be, when it was Mum's laughter not her anger that used to ring through the house. She used to laugh so hard she'd have tears in her eyes.

He goes to work. I boot my computer and upload the video. I save the Robbie clip as one file and me

143

dismantling the wall as another. I burn the Robbie clip to DVD and then stash it, unlabelled, at the bottom of my underwear drawer. Sorry, Robbie. Not the most masculine place to live.

I play the wall video through on the screen. It's almost like one of those silent movies. I mess around with the speed. Zoom through and watch the images falling like rain; slide the playhead back and watch them all jump back up into position. Typical time-wasting. I go back to the start and let it play through, and I watch myself approach the wall, climb up onto the wall, reach up for the first photo…Pause. I take a capture of the screen and dump it into Photoshop. Let it play for another few seconds, then pause again as that first print flutters to the ground. Capture, into Photoshop. And in my mind's eye, I see an image starting to form. A montage…no, a grid. Stills from the video, mixed with black and white photos. Mixed with stills from the video of Robbie, just a few scattered here and there, the idea of subliminal messages, undertones…

It takes two hours to capture and save three hundred and fifty-five images. I have the worst posture at the computer and I end up with stiff shoulders and a sore neck from hunching over the keyboard. I get up from my chair and stretch, drawing myself up onto tiptoes and rolling my shoulders, feeling the clicking and popping of stiff joints as I do. And I catch my reflection in the full-length mirror.

I've got on a pair of old trackies, cut off at the knees. I went through and massacred half of my wardrobe last year, needing something that I could wear with the leg cast. I look—like I did before—like a total dag. Only this time it's the scar I'm showing off, not the cast. My leg is pink because my weight was on it before; the white scar tissue stands out all the more.

Before I can stop myself, I reach for my SLR. It's still loaded, halfway through a roll of uninspired bush photos. I aim it at my reflection in the mirror, drop the shutter speed right down, and start to shoot. Me, then close-ups of the scar. I keep going till I reach the end of the roll of film.

I rewind it carefully and pop the back of the camera open, and the film cassette tumbles out. I weigh it in my hand, feeling the adrenaline that's kept me going through the morning die out. Leaving me once again with that feeling of being stuck, broken down on my way to somewhere.

I have a processing tank and equipment but I threw out my opened bottles of chemicals a couple of months ago because they were going off. And even if I did have the chemicals, the momentum's gone now. I stare at the computer screen, at the thumbnails of video stills, the hundreds of them, and my stomach starts to knot up again. Who was I kidding? I can't use those. I can't use any of this stuff, it won't mean anything to anyone but me.

I toss the roll of film onto my workbench and head downstairs. Mum's shut Iago outside and I let him in, let him lick me all over with sloppy kisses. He follows me into the lounge room, his claws click-clacking on the tiles, and jumps up beside me on the couch. Mum would go nuts if she knew—it's a four-thousand-dollar couch she got especially imported from somewhere. But what she doesn't know she can't complain about. I flick on the TV and we stretch out to watch. Too early for Dr Phil.

Iago stretches, nudges me with his paws. I look at him and he grins. 'So, Yago.' I scratch behind his ears and I think about the canvas and the roll of film up on my workbench. 'What are we going to do?'

We go three days basically without talking. It's not hard in our house. Mum is so rarely downstairs, and Lauren takes off most mornings, not reappearing till eight or nine at night. I don't know where she goes; whether there's friends she hangs out with, or she fills up her time with uni classes and work shifts. I can imagine her just driving as far as she can. Finding some lonely spot on top of a cliff to sit and think.

I buy three tickets to Morgan's play, hoping in some vague way it will fix things between us, but she sees right through it, and just gets mad again. 'I told you, I don't want them there.'

Still stinging from Kayla's book nerd comment, I avoid reading. I let Anthony and the guys drag me out to see a movie on Saturday night and then when I get home, I put on my running gear.

Kayla's out on her verandah again. Not smoking this time, but sitting on the steps with a bottle of beer against her left eye, the rest of the sixpack beside her. I nearly pretend I haven't seen her, but curiosity gets the better of me.

'What happened to you?'

'Got punched.'

Somehow the answer doesn't surprise me in the least. My face must reflect that, because she goes on quickly, 'At kickboxing. One of the new idiots totally botched some moves and got me in the face.'

She lowers the bottle and I can see that the left eye is actually swollen shut, and there's a dark bruise across her cheek. Though it's June she's dressed in just black leggings and a white singlet. Smelling like sweat and deodorant but, for once, not cigarettes.

I feel the tiniest shiver of adrenaline and an odd thought occurs to me. I think she might actually be quite attractive.

It throws me completely for a second. Kayla? Kayla who used to pour chocolate milk into my school bag and steal my maths homework to hand in as her own? We haven't been playmates for years and we certainly aren't friends. At the most, she's been like a weird and annoying cousin. So why am I suddenly looking at her and feeling all warm inside?

She holds up the rest of the sixpack. 'Want one?'

To venture out causes anxiety, but not to venture is to lose one's self...

'Okay.' Amazing that my voice still somehow sounds normal, because my heart is banging away madly in my chest. I've never even really thought of her as a girl before. I suppose she must have worn tight pants or short skirts around, but I never really paid much attention.

She raises an eyebrow—I've surprised her, I think—but holds out the stubby and gestures to the step beside her.

The beer is a twist top and I feel a flutter of panic in my chest at the thought that I might spectacularly crash and burn right here and now and not even be able to get the lid off. But I do, and I take a sip. I've had beer once or twice before—Aunt Jen's boyfriends usually try the male bonding thing if we meet them—but it's not like a habit. It takes a lot of concentration to pretend I know what I'm doing.

'When did Lauren get back?'

'About two weeks ago.'

She takes a drink, puts the beer down and fishes a pack of cigarettes out of her backpack. I give her a look.

'So I'm guessing I don't need to offer you one...'

'You're an idiot.' For some reason, despite the fact that I know she could flatten me with one punch, and despite the fact that my heart is still thumping away crazily, I don't even hesitate before telling her that.

'Yeah, I know.' She smiles, plays with the pack of cigarettes. Nice, straight teeth. She and I had braces at about the same time. Her hair is pretty, too. Crazy red, and all the kids at school used to make fun of her, but it's long and wavy and—*Why am I thinking these things about Kayla?*

I watch her slide the packet, untouched, back into the bag. 'I'm still trying to get Mum to quit.' I say it mildly, not wanting to derail the odd civility of our conversation.

'Yeah, good luck. She's down here bumming a smoke off me every other night.'

It's a strange thought. Two or three days could easily go by without me even seeing Mum but she's down here talking to Kayla, of all people. Is it because Kayla doesn't expect anything of her? Doesn't she realise we've pretty much given up any expectations ourselves?

We sit in silence for a while. I take small sips of beer, not sure whether I like the taste or not. What I like is that I probably look more of a man, and then I realise that if Lauren sees me she'll know that, and despise me for it utterly. Then I hate, really hate, that everything I think and do is dictated by my sister's opinion.

'How long have you done kickboxing?'

'I started after Daniel Cameron hit me in year seven. Remember that?'

I remember she called him pretentious, and he didn't

know what it meant. He got in trouble for punching her, of course, but it doesn't surprise me that Kayla went out and found her own way of making sure nothing like that ever happened again. She's not the sort of person who waits around for somebody else to fix the situation for her.

We both look up at the sound of a car coming from the end of the street, that same muffler as before and music blaring. It pulls up outside our house, a lowered Subaru. From the voices, there's at least four or five people crowded inside. The door opens and Morgan extricates herself.

'Hey, Morgs.' It's Kayla calling her, not me. She sees us. Looks surprised to see me there. Turning back to the car, she says something through the open window and the car takes off, then she turns and approaches us. She's in skinny jeans and a low-necked top that gives her more cleavage than a brother ever wants to know about. Around the house I rarely see her in anything other than school uniform or her favourite yellow hoodie, which both make her look like an oversized kid. But she's looking very grown up all of a sudden. When did she get more grown up than me?

Kayla holds out the bundle of beers. 'Want one?'

'Sure.'

'She's fifteen!' Did I squeak?

'One won't kill her. Besides, I'll be a responsible drinking partner, won't I, Morgs?'

She grins. 'You usually are.'

I watch as Kayla twists the top off and passes it to her, and I wonder how many she's already had and if I should play the parent and stop her, or not be a wuss and let her live a little. Everybody else seems to worry less and be happier for it.

So we sit there, the three of us squished together on the step. Morgan starts telling a funny story about the party she was at, and she makes us laugh, and I feel Kayla jostling and moving beside me, the warmth of her, and it makes me wish the moment won't ever end.

Later I go upstairs to Mum's room. She's huddled at her computer with a handful of used tissues spread out all around the keyboard, scrolling up through the open document.

'Mum?'

'What?'

'I've got you a ticket for Morgan's play.'

'When is it?'

'Next Friday night.'

She grimaces. 'I'm battling a cold and I still have ten thousand words to do before the end of the month. I may not have the time to spare.'

It's an excuse, and it doesn't surprise me. I'm surprised to find how much it annoys me, though.

I try to keep my voice steady. 'I think it would really mean a lot to her if you could come.'

'I'll try, but I can't make any promises. I have to meet my deadline.' Her words come impatiently, as if I'm interrupting her flow. I doubt that's the case. When she types, it's usually slowly, one finger at a time as she struggles to find the words. Like Tolstoy's exhausted Russian soldiers plodding on through the snow, just one frozen foot in front of the other because if they stop it's all over.

before
after
later

First time in my life I'm actually glad to go back to school. If Rose-Marie was looking to punish me, she succeeded spectacularly. Two weeks of precious holidays trashed. Two weeks of near-hell stuck in the house with Her Royal Highness the Self-Righteous Bitch, only getting a break from her when she took Tash out to her endless toddler activities. Not many things can make you feel as pathetic as being jealous of a two-year old's social life.

School is dull as ever but at least I can finally catch up with my friends. I'm allowed out on Thursday night for my driving lesson, which I get through without stalling and without hitting the gutter in my reverse park. Finally got all my hours up and George reckons

I'm ready to book my P's test. Some good news to take home. Terry's still avoiding me.

Rose-Marie and Terry are playing Scrabble when I get home and she doesn't even look up from the board. But Terry mutters something about coffee and leaves the room. Still pissed at me, apparently.

'Did you get a chance to look through those brochures I put in your room?' Rose-Marie. They've been there for a week, which I'll bet is what she considers the polite amount of time to let me mull over a decision like that. She knows I haven't even touched them.

'The schools?' Stupid heart pounding in my chest. 'Yeah, had a quick look. I don't mind. Somewhere local. Public is fine.'

'You didn't want to consider one of the independent schools? Livingstone is just down the road and it has an excellent reputation. Smaller class sizes, better resources...'

Livingstone School was the top brochure. I'd never even heard of it, but the picture on the front said it all. Spoilt-looking kids in miniature blazers and boater hats. Please.

Shrug. 'The public schools round here seem okay. It's only kindy to start, anyway.'

Rose-Marie's expression tells me this is the wrong thing to say. Bet Livingstone is where all the kids from her mothers' group are enrolled. She always comes home from the group with something new she's gone out and bought for Tash—the latest expensive toy or organic baby food or high-tech stroller. I don't really care either way—it's her money she's spending, and if she gets a kick out of it and Tash happens to benefit, so be it. But she's treating this school business as if it's the choice that will define the rest of Tash's life. Not sure if that scares me or just annoys me.

'I thought maybe we could take a look,' Rose-Marie presses. 'Just a quick visit, see the facilities and meet some of the staff.'

It's just a school, I want to say. I don't, because I can tell she's taking this seriously. She'll think I just don't care. Actually, I *don't* care, but I don't want her getting the shits with me, either.

'Yeah, okay.'

She nods. Maybe the fact she's won some small battle gives her the confidence to go on. 'We've been thinking, as well…What are your plans for next year?'

Next year? Be lucky if I had a plan beyond next weekend.

Shrug. 'Uni, I guess.' It's months before I have to make a decision.

'We were wondering if you might be interested in doing a gap year somewhere.'

My vague impression of gap years is that you travel overseas to work your butt off in a summer camp with whiny American kids. Or freeze it off working a ski-lift in Canada. Picture myself in the woods, standing next to a log cabin wearing sneakers and some hideous t-shirt, with Tash, in a matching ensemble, clinging to my leg.

'What would I do with Tash?'

'She'd stay here, of course.'

Whoa. Stop the train. 'What?'

Rose-Marie glances around, as if looking for backup, but Terry's not here. She looks back to me.

'Well, you couldn't take her with you…'

Meet her gaze. 'Well, I wouldn't go anywhere without her…'

A tug-of-war between us, heavy silence. Can almost see the options turning over in Rose-Marie's mind, arguments to make. She draws a breath.

'Some day you're going to want a life of your own. You'll want to go to uni, travel, get your own place, be independent…'

'You think I care about my social life more than I care about Tash?'

'You haven't given us any evidence to the contrary!'

What a low fucking blow. Part of me knows, has always known, I'm just the means to an end. Should have realised Rose-Marie would be planning life without me. Waiting for me to stuff up so she'd have a reason to get rid of me.

Stare back. 'If I go, she goes.'

I'm mad. She's mad. Her words come low, fast and dangerous. 'To what, Eliat? Where are you going to take her? You can't even look after yourself, what makes you think you can be her parent?'

'I am her parent.'

'Not the way you act.'

'So, what, just because you can afford to buy her stuff and send her to some stupid private school, you're a better parent?'

'No, being the one who stays home and changes the nappies instead of going out and getting high makes me the better parent.'

Both standing now. In each other's faces and trying to catch our breath. Tears in her eyes. I'm so full of hate for her I want to spit in her face.

I bite down on my lower lip hard, till I can taste the blood.

'She stays with me,' I manage. Before she can answer I turn and leave the room. Slam my bedroom door shut.

I don't have a bag big enough to pack everything I own. End up with rejected clothes strewn all around the room and a bag I can't zip up. Ridiculous how much crap I have, anyway. Tash's room, flipping on the light. She's asleep in her favourite position, face-down with her bottom sticking up in the air, legs tucked under her. She sits upright, groggy, looks around. Obviously something about me that scares her because the thumb goes into her mouth. Looks just like a baby again, in singlet and nappy, hair out in all directions. She scored the same dark hair as me, but her skin is lighter. Three quarters white, only one quarter Asian, at a guess. Her eyes are blue. Thanks, Jonah.

There's one of those kid-sized suitcases in the top of her wardrobe, from the time Terry and Rose-Marie took us to the Gold Coast. Right up at the top, out of my reach. I have to drag one of her toyboxes across to stand on. Manage to spill an open box of nappies all over the floor. They tumble down, hitting me on the shoulders, chest, legs as they fall.

'Shit!'

'Shit!' Tash echoes me, a small sleepy voice.

'Tash…' My warning voice. Hypocrite.

I lug the suitcase down and then pull open her drawers. Rose-Marie keeps everything tidy and organised. Singlets, shorts, skirts, jeans, play tops, pretty tops, long-sleeved tops, jumpers, pyjamas…Grab the top handful from each pile and shove them into the tiny suitcase, then head over to her shoe shelf. Nowhere near enough room in the suitcase for the tonnes of stuff Rose-Marie has bought for her.

Starting to whine. Not knowing what's going on, but the sight of me tearing her bedroom apart is obviously disturbing her.

'We're going on a holiday, you and me,' I tell her. 'What toys do you want to take?'

Won't answer me, just whines. I don't know where

to start. Spoilt kid. Dolls, Duplo, toy cars, dress-ups, building blocks…

I'm trying to shove her two favourite toy cars into the bulging suitcase when she starts to bawl. Not just cry, but scream, as if she's just fallen over or somebody's hit her. Rose-Marie must have been just outside the door. She's there within seconds. Stands in the doorway and surveys the mess. And Tash, with red face and snotty runny nose and tears everywhere, reaches out to her.

It's like somebody—no, something, like a three-tonne truck—has thumped me in the chest. Still sitting on the floor, toy cars in my hands. Feeling all the wind knocked out of me.

Making soothing noises and rubbing Tash's back, Rose-Marie steps past me, out of the bedroom. No words, no questions, just leaves.

Still sitting there when Terry comes in. Stands in the doorway and looks at me like he wants to tell me to go ahead and leave, they'll be better off without me. Quiet and grim. 'Is there a plan?'

God, I'm tired. I just stare at him. I've got nothing. Want to down a bottle of vodka and go to bed and never wake up again.

'If you're serious…You need to prove first that you really can look after her. Or else she's just going to end up back in the system. Do you want that?'

I don't know if he's just trying to provoke me or to

threaten me. Don't know if I care. I've got no energy to fight anymore.

'Go to bed. Think about what I said. We'll talk about it tomorrow.'

Saturday morning I'm up before seven. Mum made me go to bed at nine so I'd get a proper night's sleep and feel better. When it comes to health stuff there's no point arguing with Mum. At least I can understand why she feels that way.

Alan's an early bird, up most mornings at six. Mum, on the other hand, loves her sleep. She won't appear till at least nine.

He pours me coffee, then pushes the paper towards me. He's not a huge newspaper reader: he'd rather be reading the latest Tom Clancy. I glance over the page. Ads.

'What am I looking at?'

'We're going to go buy you a car.'

My stomach starts its usual dance. 'I don't want a car.'

'Half the reason your leg is taking so long to heal is because you keep overdoing it. So: drive to and from school, the cafe, wherever else it is you want to go; then you can still go walking, take Iago down into the bush, but you won't be overdoing it.'

It's a tempting argument. But it's a long way from being tempted to actually finding the guts to get behind the wheel.

He sees my hesitation and that's enough. He downs the rest of his coffee. 'The auctions start at ten. Go shower and we'll check them out.'

I don't quite know what to expect at the auctions. It's a massive shed full of cars, each with a number and key information painted on the windscreen. There are maybe a hundred or more people wandering through, checking odometers and interiors and scribbling notes.

'Where do all the cars come from?'

'A lot are ex-government or fleet vehicles, some are repossessed, and others are being sold because of damage, usually mostly minor.' We pass a dark green Mirage and Alan points at the small craters that dot the paintwork. 'Hail damage.'

My heart starts to beat a little bit faster. I move on, running my eyes over the cars, the details on the windscreen without really caring. Alan knows all about cars.

I wouldn't have the first clue.

'Anything you like?'

'You tell me.'

He shows me his top three picks, all hatchbacks or small sedans, but more expensive makes and models.

'Volvo? You buying this car for me or your mother?'

'Stronger body, better protection,' is his brief answer. I wish I hadn't asked.

The auction starts. The crowd has built to maybe two hundred, lining either side of a long driveway painted onto the concrete floor. The cars are driven up one at a time, and the auctioneer starts taking bids. Just like you see on TV, moving at an impossible speed. The first of Alan's picks comes up and the price rises rapidly. I feel him glance at me, and I say nothing, and he lets it pass. It all moves too fast for me. I don't know how serious he is about bidding or not, or how much he'd expect to pay. My leg is starting to hurt and I wish we were sitting down.

My eyes move to the back of the queue, watching a car crawl into position at the end, waiting its turn. Dark blue; totally smashed in at the front. It's a miracle it still runs. My stomach knots. No, not just that, it tightens and rolls and I think I'm going to be sick.

I grab Alan's sleeve. 'Did they bring my car here, after the crash? Did somebody buy it?'

He looks at me, eyes widening, as if it never occurred

to him that I might ask. He slips his arm around my shoulder, carefully, awkwardly, as if he wants to comfort me but feels responsible.

'Yours went to the wreckers,' he says quietly.

Of course it did. There was only half a car left by the time they cut us out. And the blood...there was blood everywhere. You'd never get it clean.

My stomach heaves and I back out of Alan's arm. I'm going to be sick if I don't get air. I'm going to throw up right here in the middle of this crowd.

I start to walk, pushing through the crowd, then move faster till I'm almost running. I get to the main doors and push out into the fresh air.

Alan's right on my heels. He finds me bent over, holding my knees, trying to breathe.

'I'm sorry.'

'It's not your fault.'

'I should have thought it through better. I forgot they had such badly damaged cars.'

We drive home in silence. I'm not mad at him, I just feel ill. Even the thought of that hail-damaged Mirage...I know the last time it hailed...

We're ten minutes from home when Alan suddenly pulls over and starts reversing back up the street. I glance behind us, wondering. 'What?' Did we hit something? I didn't feel anything.

A shiny silver Mazda hatchback sitting on a front lawn. With a For Sale sign in its window.

'No...'

'Humour me.'

He parks and gets out, strolling over to the Mazda. Obviously it makes a good first impression because he then walks all around it, starts studying the tyres, peering in through the windows. The embarrassment is enough for me to forget my nausea. Doing this at the auctions was one thing, but this is somebody's front lawn.

I try hissing his name from the car but he doesn't hear me. Reluctantly, I unbuckle my seatbelt and get out of the car.

'Come on, let's go.'

'It's five years old but it's got low k's, brand new tyres. They're asking fifteen. Pristine condition. We could probably knock them down to fourteen.'

He takes off for the front door before I get a chance to stop him. Ten minutes later we're climbing inside for a test drive.

Mum's at the kitchen table putting together a concept board when we get home. She looks up, swatches in hand.

'Where have you been?'

'We just bought a car.'

Me answering, not Alan. Somehow it hasn't shaken

me as much as I thought it would. It probably helps that I haven't had to sit in the driver's seat yet, that the car itself is still sitting out on its owner's lawn. But despite myself, I feel excitement stirring—at the prospect of owning it, if not actually driving it.

Alan reels off the details—make, model, k's and service history. 'We won't be able to get a bank cheque until Monday, but we've put a deposit down and done the REVS check.'

Mum nods. 'Well.' She puts the fabric swatches down, looks at us both, but doesn't say anything else. Annoyed? For once I can't tell. I duck out of the room before I get caught in the middle of something.

The orchid painting is still on my workbench. I pick it up, studying it critically. Okay colour mixing, nice line work; otherwise pretty average. I could hand in a bunch of similar paintings for my major work but Shepherd would probably kill me. Frankly, I wouldn't blame her. She was spot on about my architectural photos. Technically excellent. Completely soulless.

I lie the canvas back down and it knocks the film cassette, sending it rolling across the desk. I catch it before it can tumble off the edge and I hold it in my palm, wrapping my fingers over it. Such a familiar weight in my hand. And a familiar flutter, excitement and trepidation, wondering how the photos will turn out.

*

Today I bought a car. A new car. Not new new, but new to me. A new chapter. Fresh energy. Or something.

I find Alan out in the backyard. He's got his mowing clothes on, old ratty t-shirt and boardies. I dress more like him than I do Mum, who's into the designer labels and everything. I think she gets annoyed about that, wishes I was more interested in being trendy or cared about what suburb I live in. Mum's the reason we moved—the rest of us were happy in the daggy western suburbs, but once her business took off and we had enough money, she just *had* to live on the North Shore. Alan doesn't care about postcodes or appearances, but he's too easygoing to argue. I like that he doesn't sweat the unimportant stuff. I like knowing he loves me the way I am, cut-off trackies and all.

I suck in a deep breath, and try to act like it's the most natural thing in the world. 'Can I borrow your car?'

Monday. Kayla's just getting home when I head out for my jog. She got her P's a few months ago and now she's getting around in an old white station wagon. I haven't even got my L's yet. I know I should, but what then? Hour upon hour in the car with Mum, if I can even drag her away from her computer for that long. Lauren paid a fortune to get private lessons, but for her it was probably worth every cent. She and Mum wouldn't have lasted an hour.

Kayla pops the boot of the car and I pause, curious, to watch her unload. She wrangles a large sheet of wooden board—plywood, maybe, I don't know much about that stuff—out of the car and carries it towards their garage door. Repeats with a second sheet.

'Need a hand?' I don't want to sound too keen but my curiosity's piqued.

'Nah, all done.' She slams the boot closed.

'What's that for?'

'Just making stuff.'

Making what stuff? A siege engine? A medieval torture device? I wouldn't put it past her.

I think about the times I've heard the whine of power tools from her garage and assumed it was her dad at work. Maybe I was wrong.

She looks me up and down, taking in the running clothes. 'You heading out?'

'Yeah.'

'Can you hold on for a minute, and I'll come?'

It's been a few days since we hung out on the step, and I've spent it in painful internal debate, caught between the self-evident logic that there's nothing there and a sort of pathetic hope that I'm wrong. I've been craving her company but not sure what I would do once I got it. Guess I'm about to find out. I think I'm going to be sick.

She emerges from her house in the same black leggings as before, and sneakers. 'Race you to the railway bridge.'

It's a good eight hundred metres, so we set off at a jog, not a sprint. The jogging helps with the tightness in my stomach. I focus on the steady rhythm of my feet, and my breathing, and I tell myself I imagined it all.

She doesn't like me. Maybe she's just trying to be funny, or just messing with me for the sake of it. Girls do that sort of thing.

'Sorted out your uni preferences?' I ask, for something to say.

'Psychology.'

'Really?'

'Why?'

'I don't know, I just figured you'd be doing something more...' I don't even know what I was thinking, let alone how I'd put it into words without getting hit.

'Physical?' She laughs. 'No. The arse-kicking is just a hobby.' Glances at me. 'You decided yet?'

'Law at Sydney.'

She grins, but looking straight ahead, and doesn't say anything.

'What?' I think she's teasing me. I'm not sure.

'You've gone for the snobbiest thing you could find, haven't you?'

'That's what my dad studied.' It's never been a case of wanting to look smart or be academic. When I was only four or five I decided I wanted to be a lawyer like Dad. Even his disappearing from our lives didn't change that. I've never really considered doing anything else.

'I guess it'll involve plenty of books...' Now she's definitely teasing.

I reach out and punch her on the arm. I guess I probably used to chase her when we were kids, and maybe we used to push and shove each other, but if we did it's been more than ten years. Still, somehow, it surprises me how natural the instinct was. She sticks her tongue out at me, then takes off. I thought she was more mature.

The last two hundred metres are a sprint to the station. Leaves crunching under our feet, both of us panting, straining to push ahead. We reach the bridge as a train rattles past underneath, and come to a stop in the middle, under the fluorescent street lamp. We watch, trying to catch our breath, as the last few carriages of the train filter past beneath us. It'll be a while till the next one. Turramurra Station is pretty quiet.

'Beat you,' she grins, breathing deeply, fingers interlaced behind her head.

'Yeah, yeah.' I drop down onto the broken concrete path and lean against the wire mesh behind me, closing my eyes as I try to slow my breathing.

I hear her footsteps. She paces for a few more seconds, then she drops down beside me. Both of us sit there for the next minute or so, not talking, just trying to catch our breath. I'm more of a long-distance runner than a sprinter. That last hundred metres or so really took it out of me.

I open my eyes and find her watching me. Not just that, but looking me over, somehow. Smiling in a way that makes me feel like she's up to something.

'What?'

'You're cute.'

I mutter a silent thanks that my face was already red from the run. I don't know if she's teasing me or trying to hit on me or what. She grins sheepishly and turns away as if she's embarrassed, and I don't dare ask her. I don't know how I feel about it, I don't know how I'm supposed to respond. Yeah, she's attractive, but she can also be scary as hell. And unpredictable. I don't know what she'll do from one day to the next. Do I want to go there?

She jumps to her feet, shaking herself off. 'We should go, we'll get cold.'

We head back home, jogging in silence. She mutters a goodnight and disappears into her house, leaving me standing out between our two driveways, wondering.

I almost knock over Morgan coming in the front door. She follows me into the kitchen. Lauren's at the counter chopping vegetables for a stirfry.

'Where've you been?'

'Just out running.'

'With Kayla,' Morgan adds, plopping down on a bar stool.

'Seriously?' Lauren's eyes narrow.

'She and Will have a thing,' says Morgan, as if it's helpful.

'It's not a thing!' Too late, because I can feel my cheeks starting to burn.

'*Seriously?*' Lauren repeats.

'It's nothing. We just went out running, that's it.'

I feel like a fraud, a liar, as the words come from my mouth, even though I don't really know myself what's going on.

Lauren stares at me. I feel almost like she's trying to stare me down, eyes boring into me as if she's reading my thoughts. I squirm internally, feeling the stress coming off her. Did she used to be wound this tight?

'God!' Morgan bursts out. 'Who cares?' To Lauren: 'Just because you don't have any emotion doesn't mean the rest of us can't. It's about time he learned to have some fun.'

I look at Lauren, expecting an explosion. But if she's exploding, it's on the inside, jaw tightening, eyes dark and sharp. She looks down at the hand holding the knife and slowly unfurls her fingers, dropping the knife onto the chopping board. Then she steps back and pushes past me, out of the kitchen.

I find her in the bathroom. Just standing there, staring at her reflection in the mirror with a sort of dull, tired hatred.

'You need to be careful.'

'Of what?'

'Of her. Careful of getting close.'

'There's nothing—' I start to protest, but cut myself off, knowing it's pointless. Morgan's already spilled the beans. Part of me is so desperate to unload that anybody will do, even this sister. 'It's just…She's different. When I'm with her I feel like I'm actually alive.' She, more than anybody else, should understand that.

'That's what you need to be careful of. Soon as you start thinking you need somebody…It's powerful, you know. Having somebody who will hold you at night and tell you they love you…It's powerful. You'd sooner sit in that groove the rest of your life than move out of it.'

I haven't heard any of this before. It doesn't surprise me, though. It makes sense, really. It explains why she's become the way she has.

'You got out,' I point out quietly, horribly uncomfortable to be having this conversation. But grateful, I guess, to have an explanation at last.

'Yeah.' She reaches for the handtowel, wringing it between her hands as if she wants to tear it in half. 'It was like severing a limb.'

She slips past me out of the bathroom. I feel bad for my sister—and I get what she's saying—but she's probably the last person I should ever take advice from. I've spent my whole life being dictated to, pushed and pulled by her gravity like a menial planet orbiting around a blazing, relentless sun. Since she left, I've veered off on my own course without even realising. And somehow, untethered as I've been, I survived.

I wonder about what happened to her. She'll never tell me anything more than that. She wouldn't think it's my business, or that it affects anyone beyond her. The irony of it isn't lost on me; after all, Lauren's words and actions have probably done more to shape my life than anything else. Whatever happened to her has changed her, and her coming back has changed us. That's just how it works. And there's at least a small part of me that is unendingly grateful for her return, negativity and all; without it I might never have realised I'm not at her mercy anymore. That she's not the only protagonist in our story.

In my own room, I go to the window and look out. It's getting dark but before I draw the blinds I look upwards at the room I know is Kayla's. The curtains are drawn but I can see light leaking around the edges, and I wonder what she's doing, what she's thinking, whether she sees as I do the way our lives are being bumped and buffeted by the lives of those around us.

before
after
later

Mrs Perkins is the careers adviser, one of those tiny, wrinkled old people who surprise you with their intensity. Remembers everybody's name, too. Even when you drop in to her cramped office unannounced she seems to always have alarming amounts of information about you at her fingertips.

'Eliat. I was wondering when you'd come and see me.'

Last time I was there she was helping me organise my mandatory work experience. She looks at me now, eyebrows raised. Expectant. I don't know where to start.

'I need a plan.'

'Uni, TAFE or job plan?'

'Uni, I guess.'

She wants to know what subjects I do, what sort of marks I'm expecting.

'Science and maths,' she muses. 'I know we organised your work experience in a pathologist's lab. Is that the sort of thing you're leaning towards? Or medicine generally? You've set yourself up with the right subjects.'

Doctor Eliat Singleton: it's got a ring to it. A completely implausible one. With Tash…

Mrs Perkins reads my face. 'No? What, then? This is your chance to choose. What do you want to do?'

It feels like too personal a question. Maybe that's because I've only ever had one ambition bigger than myself.

'Something to do with brains?'

My answer doesn't faze her one bit. 'What specifically? Psychology? Psychiatry? Or are we talking neuroscience of some sort?'

Problem is, I'm not sure. I don't know which rock to look under first. 'Something to do with how people remember, how they store memories…I just think that stuff is really interesting.'

I guess she's heard weirder things. She nods, flips expertly through her UAC guide. 'I know New South has Neuroscience as part of their Advanced Science degree…'

I leave with a list of options and a contact number for somebody at the university who works in Alzheimer's research. Not exactly what I'm after, but it's a start. And I can feel something. A sense of not being quite so hopeless.

Don't have the courage to ask Rose-Marie how last night has affected the new rules, so I stay in Friday night. An exercise in arse-kissing, pretty much. An hour and a half playing with Tash, not just chase and tickle, but matching up those cards that Rose-Marie bought to teach Tash her numbers, and then we build a zoo using her plastic animals and wooden blocks. I can feel Rose-Marie's eyes boring into the back of my neck the whole time, as if she thinks I'm just putting it on for her benefit. Maybe I am. I never feel completely natural with Tash when Rose-Marie is around. Always feel like I'm faking it. Pretending to be the parent she wants me to be instead of just being myself. Guess I've known from the start that just being myself was never going to cut it with these two.

I do my homework and then do the ironing without being asked. In bed, pyjamas and all, by half past ten. Izzy'll just be warming up for the night.

In my bed, grab my laptop and rest it against my knees. Ready at any second to hide the laptop under the covers and pretend to be asleep, I start to go through the different university options I got from Mrs Perkins. It's overwhelming.

Terry and Rose-Marie head to bed just before eleven,

when their movie finishes. Half close the laptop lid, wait and listen for the footsteps on the stairs. Five minutes: nothing. Not sure whether I expect them to be keeping their distance or keeping a closer eye on me. In the end I guess I really don't expect them to care.

Another couple of hours Googling and reading articles online about cognitive neuroscience, memory and infantile amnesia. Some stuff I haven't read before. None of it answers my questions, just keeps me wondering. Read until I can't keep my eyes open any longer. None of the usual shitty mind-games, at least for one night.

Most of Saturday morning I spend actively avoiding being in the same room as either of them. The silence makes my teeth itch, and neither of them seems particularly keen to be around me anyway. Terry even takes himself off to play golf, which I know he hates. Whatever it takes to get away from me, apparently.

By afternoon I'm sick of being housebound. I test the waters, ask Rose-Marie if I can go hang out with April for a couple of hours. Either she's tired of me being around the house or else she's giving me enough rope, because she says yes. Besides, it's a chance to exercise authority: dinner at home first and then I have to be home by nine-thirty.

Izzy is disgusted. 'How are you supposed to have any fun and still be home by nine-thirty?'

Sit on her bed and watch her straighten her long foiled locks. Stupid, vain, blonde Izzy. But I don't have anyone else.

When I tell her about the fight, she immediately jumps to my defence. 'That's stupid. She's not their kid, she's yours.'

'Yeah, I know…' Hear the doubt in my own voice.

She waves the straightener in my face. 'Don't tell me you agree with them.'

I know she'll take my side, because she's loyal and stubborn, but I'm not sure if I want her to.

'They've done a lot for her…'

She pulls a baggie out of her desk drawer and chucks it at me. 'That's the end of it. You need it more than I do.'

I catch it, but then put it down. Shake my head.

'They've really done a number on your head, haven't they?'

I can't explain it. This whole week has got out of control and all of a sudden I just feel tired of my life, the battle between who I am and who they want me to be. I hate having to act fake, pretend I would really spend hours doing mnemonics with Tash even if Rose-Marie wasn't there watching. But I want to get on top of stuff, too. I want to feel clean. I'm tired.

Terry's stretched out on the couch, tuned to the weather channel. On the screen is a spiralling cloud floating across the Pacific Ocean, Terry's low-pressure system on its way. Rose-Marie's sitting at the kitchen counter, stitching a button back onto Tash's red overalls. Got her glasses on to see. They make her look closer to her actual age. The way she dresses, acts and talks, you'd think she was in her mid-thirties. She's actually forty-five. Terry's nearly fifty.

'How was April?' She's trying to be civil.

I'm trying to sound natural. 'Still crying her guts out over a boy. She'll be all right. She was too good for him anyway.'

Terry lifts his head to look at me. Cocks an eyebrow. 'I thought you said she was fighting with her parents.'

Just being a good listener? Or trying to catch me out? I don't know. He's looking at me like he doesn't trust me one bit.

'Yeah, she was going out with this guy who was twenty-five.' Words roll off my tongue smoothly, almost without thinking. Too easy. 'They made her break it off, kept saying he was too old for her.'

'Twenty-five is too old.'

Shrug. 'Not saying I disagree.'

Silence. Suddenly I get the feeling they've been talking about me. Wondering what I'm really doing, if they can trust me, if they can believe a word I say. Sometimes I don't even know why I say half the rubbish I do. It'd be so much easier if I didn't have to remember my own bullshit the whole time. Mostly it's just habit.

Terry flips off the TV and leaves the room. I watch

him go, wondering how long he's going to be mad with me. Not the forgiving sort, apparently.

'We were thinking of going into the art gallery tomorrow to see the Whitely retrospective. It's the last day. Are you right with Tash?'

It's an offhand request that screams *test*. I just nod. Match Rose-Marie's tone. 'Yeah, I'll take her to a park or something. She's getting good with the soccer ball.'

She ties off the thread and folds the overalls. She'd never think to make me do a job like that, just does it all herself. So why is it my fault? Resentment rises up in me. Collides with all the guilt that's already churning around. Before I know it I'm saying, 'Is Terry planning to just ignore me forever?'

Rose-Marie seems annoyed still, impatient, but at least she's not just walking out. Could she possibly be feeling at all guilty about the things she said? Not sure. She can be pretty damn self-righteous.

'He's disappointed,' she says stiffly.

'I made a mista—'

'No.' She interrupts, irritated that I'm trying to brush her words away. 'Really. He believed in you. He's invested just as much in you as he has in Tash, probably more, and what you did was a real slap in the face.' Angry tears in her eyes again. Grey-green eyes and the light reflecting off her glasses. The intensity in her voice makes me feel like something is wrapping itself around me, tighter and tighter.

'We took you in! Do you know what a big step that was for us? We're the ones who used to have a social life! We traded that in for a screaming baby and checking on homework.'

Bull. Shit. 'You didn't want me, you just wanted Tash.'

'We took both of you in. We took on the role of parents to both of you. And all this time we thought we were doing a good job. *We* thought we had some sort of a family here.' She grabs a tissue and blows her nose. 'Apparently we were wrong.'

A tightening feeling. Hands closing around my chest. Squeezing the air out. Don't know if she's trying to manipulate me but even if she is, I'd swear she's really hurt. And I don't know if I actually care, or if I only care about how it makes me feel. Why the hell did she have to use the f-word?

Rose-Marie slides off the stool, overalls in one hand, sewing kit in the other. 'That's why we're mad.'

In the bedroom I wake up my laptop and start to type out a list. Chronological, starting with Mike and Debbie Adderley. I know my records inside out. Including siblings and school friends, it comes to forty-eight names. I scroll back to the top, and highlight the first name.

Mike Adderley. I was with them for just under six months before I got shifted to what was supposed to be a more permanent situation. All I remember about him is from a photo. Long, tanned arms and legs, and a scruffy mullet which apparently I used to like pulling on. I hit delete.

It takes me an hour to work my way through the list, deleting names one at a time. Combing my brain each time for memories, waiting to feel something. Nothing. From a list of forty-eight I end up with four. Rose-Marie, Terry, Tash, Izzy. I skip down to the last name and highlight it, searching for something in me that tells me to stop. Nothing does. Delete. No hesitation, no regret, maybe even the slightest sense of satisfaction, like peeling off dirty clothes. Scroll back up. Rose-Marie. Trying to summon up a memory of affection for her, but nothing comes, just her inane questions, her fake smile. Delete.

Terry's harder. I like him. We get along. But turns out he's just as judgmental as Rose-Marie, pig-headed and unforgiving. If I think ahead, imagine myself somewhere else, it's a relief to be free from that. Delete.

One name left. And as I think of her, the image that comes into my mind is of her screaming on her bed. Reaching out. Not to me, but to Rose-Marie.

later

This time he calls me.

'You checking up on me?' I ask, cocking an eyebrow as I drop down into my seat at the cafe table.

'You need somebody to keep an eye on you,' he announces with mock seriousness. He gestures to the car keys in my hand. 'You drove?'

I can't help myself; I grin. 'Yeah. I got a new car.'

He nods approval. 'Congratulations.'

I tell him about Alan dragging me to the auctions, about buying the Mazda, about getting in the driver's seat again. When I got to the shops it turned out that my usual camera store didn't have any processing chemicals in stock, but somehow that didn't even really matter. I got myself a strawberry shake from Macca's and wandered through the shopping centre for an hour or so, looking at the puppies in the pet shop window and snorting to myself at the latest fashions in the endless clothing stores. Feeling like my old self again. When I got home Alan was mowing the front strip. Waiting for me, I'll bet. He'd offered to come along for the ride and I nearly gave in and let him, but then I stopped myself, knowing I'd probably chicken out twenty metres down the road and make him drive instead.

'How's it going?' says Daniel.

'Pretty good, I think.' It only took me a few minutes to remember how it all worked, first in Alan's car and then in the new Mazda. Muscle memory. Into gear, handbrake off, gentle acceleration...In a way, deceptively easy, harmless. Before it all happened I never really thought about how much damage could be done with something so ordinary.

Alan said the driver of the other car tried to come visit me, but Mum screamed and shouted that idea down pretty quickly. I don't blame her at all. I do sometimes wonder, though: what do you say to someone after something like that? When you were just minding your own business and ended up killing someone? The guilt must be horrible.

'I can't hate them, you know.'

Daniel looks at me, quizzical.

'The driver of the other car. It was an accident. It's not like they were drunk or speeding or anything...It was just dark, and the lights were out, and they forgot to put on their headlights...'

I realise I feel, irrationally, that I'm the one who should be saying sorry. Sorry that now they have to live with the guilt of what they did.

I can feel the heaviness starting to creep back into my chest, threatening to take over again, drag me back down. I shake my head to clear it away. No. Time to change the subject.

'Any action on the romance front?'

He cracks a smile. 'Didn't your parents teach you how to mind your own business?'

'No. My Mum's Italian. Do I need to explain how that works?'

Another smile. He starts to speak but then stops himself. There's a look on his face that I recognise from years and years ago, when Mum started dating Alan.

'There is!' I crow. Maybe it's because I can't get a boy to even look in my direction, or maybe it's just because he seems like such a decent guy. I want good things for him. I want him to feel like I do—that there's hope.

He's amused, maybe a bit embarrassed by the fuss I'm making.

'Who is it?' I demand, dying of curiosity. 'She'd better not be some blonde airhead.'

He feigns hurt. 'You think I would be so shallow?'

'No.' I can't even pretend to believe it. 'She's probably working on a cure for cancer or something, right? Or working with orphans in Africa…' I trail off, suddenly struck by a thought. 'It's not her, is it? The girl you broke up with after my accident? Lauren?'

He looks away, and that's my answer.

'Is it serious?' I'm not judging him, just curious.

'It's not anything, just yet. I haven't even seen her in person since…you know. But we've been emailing, just chatting about things. She's continuing her degree in New Zealand, and she's looking at doing some volunteer work during her next break.'

'Working with orphans in Africa.' It's a statement, not a question, because his look has already given the answer away. 'You reckon it'll work out this time?'

'I have no idea.'

'I hope it does.' I mean it, I really do. And from the way he nods, I know that's what he's thinking too.

The box of photography supplies arrives on Monday; I had to have it shipped from Melbourne. I slice it open and dig through the packing peanuts to unearth the fixer and film developer bottles and the extra roll of bulk film I ordered.

Just like driving, it all comes back to me: hands working blind in my black bag to get the film into the processing tank; chemicals mixed and measured; processing tank agitated. It's calming, knowing exactly what I'm doing, confident of how it should turn out.

Done. I stand back to survey my strip of negatives as

they hang in the window, fluttering in the slight breeze. I grab another peg and clip it on the bottom to weigh the film down so it doesn't curl up as it dries.

'How do they look?'

Alan's always been a big fan of everything I do, especially my photos. Every time I showed him my processed negatives for the first time or produced a final print he'd study it and smile and tell me I had a knack. I've never taken that for granted. Mum's so wrapped up in her own world I'd pretty much have to shove something in her face before she noticed it.

I study them. 'All right.' The top lot of photos are all leaves and squiggly bark gum trees. Aesthetically speaking, they're nicely composed, capturing interesting shapes and textures. Critically speaking, they're boring. Lifeless. The rest of the roll, on the other hand...The sun was coming in from the window on my left, and it throws sharp shadows. My expression from behind the camera is serious, focused. It's going to be intense.

He leans in closer to look at them properly. 'For school?'

'Yeah.'

He studies the lower half of the roll. Me and my scar. I realise I'm holding my breath as I watch him, not because I'm afraid he'll get mad like Mum might, but that he might not understand. But he's got a good poker face. It doesn't give much away.

He draws back. 'How's your car going?'

He's not really asking about the car, but he's good at being tactful. I take a moment to think. I haven't really let myself analyse it too much.

'It's all right, actually. It just feels...I don't know. Weird, but normal.' Like the last nine months hasn't happened. Except for the fact that I've been taking the long way round so that I haven't had to go through any major intersections.

He squeezes my shoulder. 'I'm proud of you.'

He's always been careful about physical touch, especially since I hit adolescence. He'll always give me pats on the back or squeeze my arm or something. I know it doesn't mean he doesn't love me. I just think he's had so much child protection stuff drilled into him over the years, and had to investigate enough of that sort of thing, especially between children and their stepfathers, that he's learned to play it safe, not start anything that could be misinterpreted.

But stuff that. I know he's a decent guy, and he's my dad. I hug him, and I realise as I do that it's been a long time, maybe since Robbie died, or even before that.

'Thanks for making me do it.' It. Not just the film, but the car thing. And everything, really.

'Me? I didn't make you do anything. You're the one who accosted me and demanded to borrow my car.'

I can hear the smile in his voice, and it makes me smile. 'Shut up.'

When my negatives are dry I carefully cut them up

and put them into a sleeve, ready to enlarge at school. In my mind I can already see the finished product, the grid of images on a white gallery wall. The snapshots taken from the videos, the photos of me and my scar… quotes, maybe, on 6x4 cards. Maybe even some of the torn-up photos, if I haven't chucked the bag of them out yet. I'd have to mount the whole thing somehow, for presentation at school. MDF sheets, painted white. Got to double-check the size limits…

I can almost see the cogs and wheels in my mind, or at least the creative part of it, starting to churn and cough. Like a machine that's been lying dormant, gathering dust.

I know what to do. It's crazy the sheer relief I feel at that realisation, like I've finally picked myself up and I'm back in motion. I know what to do.

Wednesday is opening night. I'm still awake when Morgan gets dropped home afterwards. I find her in the kitchen, face still caked with theatre makeup, making herself a tinned-spaghetti sandwich.

'How'd it go?'

'All right.'

'Did people like it?'

A shrug. 'They clapped. But what else are they going to do?'

I can't quite figure out if she's acting nonchalant or truly doesn't care. I can't quite believe that after all these weeks of rehearsals she doesn't have more to say. Maybe she thinks I don't really want to hear, that I'm just asking out of obligation.

'How'd your backdrops go?'

Another shrug, and she takes a bite of the sandwich. Spaghetti sauce drips down her chin and she wipes it away with the back of her hand. Around a mouthful of food: 'Okay.'

Anthony, at school in the morning, is far more vocal. I get a detailed rundown on who was good, who was bad, who stepped on other people's cues. 'Lucy Smithers accidentally walked off-stage halfway through a scene. Morgan had to drag her back on stage and adlib the whole thing till Lucy figured out what the hell was going on. She was pretty good at it, actually. Pulled it off with some thees and thous.'

Good at making stuff up on the spot? I'm not ultra-surprised. Morgan's been known to wriggle out of some tight spots with fast talking. She doesn't exactly hang with the best crowd at school.

'She didn't seem very happy with how it went...'

'That's because your sister is a born director. You should have seen her during rehearsals. She knows every line inside out, every cue and movement inside out. Better than Lordley, even.'

Anthony is sometimes too frank, but he never shirks from giving credit where credit is due. I feel a slight swell of pride inside for Morgan, but it's tempered by a guilty awareness. I didn't really think she had it in her.

She doesn't get in till nearly eleven. I don't know

whether she was at rehearsals or just hanging out with friends. If Lauren was home, she'd be asking, but I haven't seen her since this morning. I made some lasagne and sat down to eat it by myself in my room with a book, because anywhere else in the house feels too empty.

Morgan stands in my doorway, poking suspiciously at a reheated plateful with a fork. 'Did you use cubed cheese in this?'

'No, it just all stuck together when I cooked it.'

'You put too much in, that's why.'

Morgan's the chef, not me. I wouldn't normally bother making something so complicated, except I needed something to distract me. Even then, I couldn't stop wondering about Morgan and worrying about the play, and then worrying about Kayla, and what she said and whether I blew it somehow because she hasn't spoken to me since, hasn't even looked my way. And about Dad, who has a new life but for some reason wants to be a part of ours again…

'Are you coming home tomorrow afternoon?'

'No, I want to fix the forest backdrop. It's too bright at the top, the sky needs to be darker.'

I hesitate, then go for it. 'I don't know if Lauren or Mum is coming.'

'I already told you, I don't want them there. They'll just ruin it.'

'Anthony says you're really good. I think Mum'll want to see it.'

'I could break a leg and Mum wouldn't notice. She's not interested in what I do.' It's an offhand statement, not deliberately self-pitying, but you can hear the trace of bitterness in it nonetheless. Same way Lauren would talk. Would I?

She disappears into her bedroom. I get ready for bed and pull the covers over me but don't turn off the light yet. I feel uneasy about Lauren. Her words, and the image of her standing there in the bathroom, wringing that handtowel, keep coming back to me. I flip through the half-dozen books on my bedside table, not able to read more than a page at a time of any of them.

I hear footsteps on the stairs at quarter to one. Not somebody going up, but Mum coming down, probably to grab some food. She likes to write into the small hours of the morning. I guess it's when the house is quiet. Not that we ever really make much noise. Maybe it's the feeling of isolation she feeds off.

I lay my book down gently and reach to push the covers off me, then I stop, and just listen. The fridge opening and closing. The clink of a plate gently touching the granite benchtop, then the softer sound of the plastic container with the leftover lasagne. She won't bother reheating it. I have one memory of Mum, from when I was only four or five, and she was drinking wine and eating chocolate cake at my cousin's wedding, and laughing and enjoying herself and the food. Lauren and Morgan must have been running around somewhere else, because I was sitting on her lap, and she offered me some of the cake, dark chocolate with French chocolate cream fill, and then gave me a sip of the sweet dessert wine. That's my one memory of her enjoying food. Now she lives on leftovers, those awful microwaveable dinners and instant coffee, and I don't think she even cares.

I tug the covers back up over me, wriggle back down on my pillows and reach for the light. A flick of the switch and the room is plunged into darkness. I lie there silently, listening to her footfalls as she ascends the staircase, and a sort of helpless sorrow overtakes me, a sense of quiet despair.

Not for myself, but for Mum, for Lauren. Part of me wants to cry, but the tears that seem to be rising up reach my chest and stay there, clogging it, making it feel tight, and I lie there awake and dry-eyed.

Friday afternoon when I get home from school, there's still no sign of Lauren. I know Mum's home but I can't hear anything from upstairs. At five-thirty, I venture halfway up the stairs before stopping and turning back. At six I get to the landing but can't find the courage to knock. At half past, I do, and when she doesn't answer I nudge the door open to find the room dark. She's stretched out on top of the covers in her dressing gown, sound asleep.

I stand there and watch her for a long second, not surprised. Disappointed, but only by myself, that I actually thought for once she might come through. Feeling like I've let Morgan down somehow, by failing in this.

I know Kayla is home because her car is in their driveway. I can hear the whine of power tools coming from their garage and head that way cautiously. The roller door is open a little at the bottom, and I glance under, seeing familiar black Converse across the floor.

Feeling a little like I'm trespassing, I grab the bottom of the door and slide it higher. It squeaks a little in the channels, but retracts fully without resistance. I find Kayla staring at me, decked out in protective goggles and dust mask, what looks like a power sander in hand. She's surrounded by pieces of wood on sawhorses and propped up against walls.

'Hi,' she says, raising a quizzical eyebrow. I feel a bit stupid just showing up, and for a long second I wonder if I've just imagined whatever it is that's happened between us. At school she hasn't been treating me any different to how she used to, which is effectively as if I don't exist.

Is she embarrassed? Is she pretending she doesn't know me at school because she's worried about what her friends will think?

These are the questions that have been swirling around in my head, but as I meet her gaze I find I don't even really care what the answer to them is, because right now I'm thinking about Morgan thinking nobody even cared enough to come.

'Will you come to Morgan's play with me?'

The eyebrow is raised higher. She pulls the goggles and mask off with one hand, but doesn't put the tool down, as if she needs to stay armed. 'Are you asking me on a date?'

Am I? I hadn't really thought through the semantics of it. I feel strangely detached from the situation, as if I could do the impossible. 'I'm asking you to come see Morgan's play. I have spare tickets.'

She shifts the weight of the sander from one hand to the other, as if mulling it over. 'Only if you ask me properly.'

I'm not good at playing games. I don't understand why girls do it. I'm pretty sure this is some big joke to her, that she'll go into school tomorrow laughing about it. But even that fear is dulled, somehow. I have to do this one thing right for Morgan. 'What do you want me to say?' I ask, resigned.

'Ask me on a date.'

'Why?' The question, stupid as it is, escapes my mouth before I can stop it.

'Because that's what boys do.'

I've gone so far that it's really too late to back out, I realise. So I might as well just get it over with. I draw in a deep breath. 'Will you come to Morgan's play with me...as a date?'

She tilts her head to the side as if considering taunting me. The sander changes hands again. Then she nods, placing it on a shelf to the side. When she turns back to face me, I'm half expecting a smile, but instead her expression is serious. Not sullen or watchful like she often puts on, but serious, as if she's allowing me to see the real her. And she just says, 'Okay.'

before
after
later

All right, Terry: here we go. I start proving myself. Pick up Tash every afternoon, entertain her, do my homework and study for the upcoming half-yearlies, do the washing or dishes without having to be asked. Go for my P's test and pass. At night I sit in bed with my laptop and research the things I need: financial support from the government, childcare subsidies, the rental market, second-hand cars. Every day seems to suck more out of me, making me emptier. Like the country, I'm in drought, getting drier by the day and hoping for rain that might never come.

Terry's low-pressure system's still playing hard to get, loitering on the east coast of the TV weather map, dangling promises of a breakthrough. The tight feeling in my chest doesn't go away either. I avoid Terry and Rose-Marie, almost more worried that they will forgive me than that they won't. Although it doesn't seem likely in the near future, if our frosty exchanges are anything to go by. They're suspicious of Good Eliat. Sceptical.

'I can do it.' Tash's words coming from my mouth. Rose-Marie's reminded me Tash is due for a vaccination and offered to take her to the doctor. Rose-Marie just nods, acknowledges it. Next morning I'm woken at five-thirty by Tash climbing on top of me. Rose-Marie and Terry have shut their bedroom door, blocking her from waking them.

It's like a tiny war. Every day there's another job, another responsibility that Rose-Marie pushes onto me. I can fight back by doing it better than her without letting her see me struggle.

Monday. Groan as the full weight of a two-year-old body yanks me from my sleep. 'Go back to bed.' Still dark. Don't understand that kid's body clock. She's demanding breakfast, when it's too early even for the early news. Struggle to keep myself from falling asleep again. Flip between infomercials, aerobics and some religious program while Tash chews on dry Froot Loops. Makes me stop on the aerobics channel. Dances around the living room, trying to do the moves. Drops Froot Loops all over the carpet and manages to crush one or two under her bare feet. 'Tash!'

Vacuum up the mess before she can spread it any more. Put away the Froot Loops. 'You shouldn't eat that crap anyway.'

'More.' I was up till two studying for my English and biology half-yearlies. The sun is only now starting to come up, and it feels like I've had no sleep at all.

'No, you made a mess. You can have some juice, but you have to be careful.'

Leave her playing with her cars while I have my shower. Return to find her with one of Rose-Marie's DVDs in one hand and her bottle of juice in the other. 'What the hell are you doing?'

Sex and the City is covered in sticky fingerprints. The DVD drive is jammed open with a Wiggles disc.

'You don't touch that! You know that. Mum does it for you, or Rose-Marie or Terry.'

I pry The Wiggles free. The disc tray hesitates, then whirs and retracts. The DVD has a scratch on it from her manhandling. 'Shit.'

'Shit,' Tash echoes me.

'Stop it!'

By the time we're on the bus she's gone quiet. Head lolls on my shoulder, thumb in her mouth as if the sugar has worn off. Drop her off just past seven, first child of the day. Gate shuts behind me and all I want is to sink to the ground and burst into exhausted tears.

Instead, I walk. It's four or five k's to school. Every time my mind starts to get into gear I push my legs that little bit faster, mutter *Othello* quotes as fast as I can, talk myself through themes.

The Gloria Jean's five minutes from school is the favoured place for the latte crowd, but not this early. I'm the only student in the place. Everybody else is dressed in suits, looking busy and confident. The way I feel on a Saturday night—knowing what's going to happen, ready to take on the world. Not how I feel right now.

Sit at a table in the corner and hold the mug between my hands and try not to feel like this is the day that my world will cave in once and for all. Watch the familiar weather icons on the flat-screen TV in the corner and feel like Terry's low-pressure system is coming for me, judge, jury and executioner.

English exam is at nine. I end up sitting across the aisle from April. She gives me a nervous grin and I half smile back, wondering what she would really think of me if she knew what she's got up to in all the stories I've told Terry and Rose-Marie.

Usually in exams I don't have problems with focus: I fall into the rhythm of scratching pens and write until I'm out of time. But right now I'm wishing for a drink, something to settle my mind, which wants to go in every direction other than the one I need it to.

Start the *Othello* essay. Hit a dead end and switch

to the creative writing. Plough through that for maybe half a page before realising I'm writing complete crap. Screw the paper up and go back to *Othello*. By the end of three hours I've managed about five full pages altogether, if I'm lucky. If it makes sense, I might just pass. If it doesn't, I'm done for.

Izzy catches up with me as we escape from the hall. 'That was torture.'

'I need a drink.'

'Thought you'd crossed over to the sober side?'

'I just need one drink.'

'It's the needing bit that makes it a problem.'

'Shut up.'

Don't even bother trying to cram for bio. A one-hour break and my brain is rejecting any attempt to think. I stretch out on the grass next to the oval and let Izzy talk rubbish.

Then we're back in the claustrophobic silence of the hall. Mrs Williams presiding. I tune out while she goes over the exam layout, which is pure rebellion, really. It's only when the clock starts that I actually tune back in, pull the exam towards me and flip it open.

The multiple-choice questions are easy. I'm almost done with them when the door at the side of the hall groans open. Every student looks up: Mrs Clegg from the office with a cordless phone in her hand. Even before anybody looks in my direction I know it's for me.

Two multiple-choice to go. Punnet squares, of course. I force my eyes back onto the paper and my mind onto the questions, as if it's the last precious minute of the exam. But the words are suddenly meaningless. The click-clacking of Mrs Clegg's heels. A light touch on my shoulder. 'Eliat.'

It's Teresa from Tash's childcare centre. Tash has a temperature. They've tried Panadol and damp towels but her temperature hasn't dropped enough.

I might not know everything but I know this partic-ular policy. Rose-Marie made me read through all the paperwork from the childcare centre when we first put Tash in. They have an hour from the time the tempera-ture is first recorded. If it's still too high at the end of the hour and nobody has picked Tash up, the policy is to call an ambulance.

'Did you already try Rose-Marie? And Terry?'

'Rose-Marie is stuck at work. She said you should be able.'

Stuck at work my arse. She's just seized a chance to make things harder for me. If I made them call her again, or Terry…But if I do…

We wait our turn at the doctors' surgery. There's a few other kids here, playing in the corner with the pile of toys. Tash is slouched on my lap, thumb in her mouth again. She was crying when I picked her up. I'm slouched too, arm looped loosely around her.

I'm handed a script to get filled. It's most likely a run-of-the-mill virus.

It takes an hour and three buses to get to the pharmacy and then get home, and Tash whinges the whole way. The medicine is cherry flavoured but I still have to almost force it down her throat. Lies on the lounge sucking on her thumb, red-faced and snot-nosed, and watches her Wiggles DVD.

My phone, on silent on the kitchen bench, buzzes at ten-minute intervals. Izzy trying to call me. After an hour of watching it I give in and answer.

'What?'

'What happened?'

'I don't want to talk about it.'

She's the best and worst of friends at a time like this, refusing to take no for an answer. 'I'm coming over,' she announces, and she hangs up.

Turns up at the door with a bottle of tequila in hand. Part of me is thankful to have company. The rest of me marvels at her idiocy. Sometimes she just doesn't get it.

'Are you stupid? I've got Tash.'

Shrugs, tucks it behind her back. 'Just in case. So what do you want to do?'

Look past her to the dented nineties BMW parked

crookedly in the no-parking zone, bright plastic P-plate jammed in beside the number plate. Her parents bought it when she threatened to drop out of school last year. If she gets through the HSC, it's hers to keep. If.

'Can we just drive somewhere?'

'Where?'

'Anywhere.'

There's a spare booster seat for Tash in the garage. I spend ten minutes doubled over in Izzy's back seat trying to remember how to anchor it in properly. Tash has fallen asleep on the couch and she's grumpy when I wake her. Kicks up a fuss about being put in the car seat and chucks her Tippee cup at me. Izzy puts on a dance track for her. 'How's that? Or do you want Britney?'

Ten minutes later she's sound asleep again, thumb back in mouth, cheeks flushed. I can't help feeling edgy. Part of me wonders what Izzy would say if I asked her to drive and drive and not turn back. Part of me wishes I had those two packed suitcases in the boot.

'So where are we going?'

My answer comes completely out of the blue, but suddenly it's the only thing that makes sense. 'Singleton.'

'Singleton like your last name?'

'Just head north.'

We don't talk much. Izzy tries to start up conversation a few times. I don't give her much to work with. Stare at the city passing by, then the suburbs, then the massive sandstone walling us in as we speed along the freeway.

'How far is it?'

'I'll let you know.'

We drive for nearly three hours. Tash is completely out of it. When we finally stop in the town centre it takes a while to rouse her. She looks around, bleary-eyed. Her hair is sweaty and flattened from sleeping in the car seat. The medicine must be wearing off; she's a ball of heat as I lift her up and hold her against me.

Izzy climbs out and looks at me across the top of the car as she stretches. 'Okay, now do you want to fill me in?'

The Coles supermarket logo shines brightly against the dusky sky. Tail end of peak hour, or as close as it gets here. People are bustling around, but to me everything just seems to have stopped.

'What?' Izzy prods, halfway between exasperated and freaked out. 'What are we doing here?'

'Let's go in.'

'What are we getting?'

Look at my watch. Just past six. 'Dinner. And some stuff for Tash.'

Bright and buzzing and not quite real. Fluoro lights and packed shelves and screaming specials. I send Izzy to find us something to eat and take Tash with me looking for Panadol. She's starting to whinge, rubbing at her face and her ears like she does when she's tired or sick. I don't have a thermometer but can tell just from holding her that her temperature's back. Seems worse than before.

'Yeah, I know, I know. I'm finding the medicine, okay?'

The medical section is at the very end of aisle nine. I find the children's Panadol and go in search of Izzy. Then I stop.

The frozen food section is spread out in front of me, along the back wall of the building. Brightly lit cabinets full of frozen peas and pizza and ice-cream.

Everything goes fuzzy. The humming, buzzing sound of the freezers fills my ears. The lights dim a little. Tash is a heavy weight in my arms.

Eyes on the freezers. Let her slide to the ground. Aware of her reaching back up for me, starting to cry. It's as if I'm underwater. I don't even look at her. Glimpses of sound, of smell, the tipping point of memory…I'm close to it. A swell of confusion, of lostness…

'Eliat!'

Izzy's voice. The world starts to come back into focus. Tash pulling at my leg, crying. Iz stares at me.

'What's wrong with you?'

Can't answer her. I nearly had it…My mind scrambles to catch hold of the last traces.

No. It's gone.

Izzy takes charge. Picks up Tash and nudges me with

the bag of Doritos in her hand. 'We're going.'

She pays. Manages, somehow, to strap Tash into the car seat. I drop into the passenger seat and pull my seatbelt on.

Still numb, I flip down the sunvisor. Stare at my reflection in the tiny mirror. Dark eyes stare back at me. Near-black but still shaped like a Caucasian's. My hair still holds a few curls from my efforts this morning, but otherwise it's straight and limp. Asian father, white mother. Asian mother, white father? That's the question, and I'm even guessing about that. But I can't get rid of it no matter how hard I try.

I was named after a woman named Eliat Smith. Don't know who named her or where the name came from. I hate it. I've always hated it.

Eliat Smith found me one day in the freezer aisle in the Singleton Coles. Not crying, but sitting on the floor clutching a stuffed yellow bunny rabbit and scowling furiously at everyone who walked past through an untidy black fringe. Or that's the way she told it.

Nobody knew who I was. Nobody knew where I had come from. And sixteen years and a dozen lifetimes later, nothing has changed.

The darkroom is empty. I feel cheated somehow by Morgan's absence, though it would be a fair exchange for mine on Friday. Friday, which seems another lifetime ago.

I have art just before lunch and I stay in the darkroom right through to produce four proper prints. I don't dare leave them in the drying racks—things get lost and ripped up when the junior classes come in here—so I take the final prints out into the classroom to dry them with the hairdryer.

Sarah Bancroft.

She's bent over the desk, a fine brush in her hand and ink bottles spread out on the desk. I can't see what she's actually painting but from the slow, careful movements I can tell it must be meticulous.

I move closer and she looks up, hand mid-air. A moment of unmasked surprise at the interruption, then the habitual scowl—habitual at least as far as I'm concerned—drops into place.

'What are you doing here?'

'I was working in the darkroom.' I'm suddenly conscious not just that I'm holding the prints, but of the subject matter. I move across to another desk and lay them flat so that she can't see them. As I do I catch a glimpse of her painting.

A portrait of a woman. A damn impressive one at that. If I wasn't looking at the ink and brush in her hand I would have easily believed it was a black and white photograph.

I can't help myself. I'm curious. 'Who is that?'

She looks at me, a long, cold stare. Then, without saying anything, returns to her work. Ouch.

I shake my prints for a few seconds to try to get rid of excess water, then fire up the hairdryer. Bancroft is dipping her brush into the ink and she jumps at the sound, knocking the bottle right over. Ink gurgles out, pools on the desk.

'Shit!'

She grabs her art paper and lifts it right up off the desk, before the spreading ink reaches it. It runs towards the edge of the table and she backs right up, moving away just as it starts to drip onto the floor.

'Sorry.' I shift the hairdryer onto a quieter setting. 'My bad.'

'You could have ruined my portrait!'

'And I said sorry. I apologised. What more do you want?' I honestly would have felt bad if that had happened. But the portrait is fine. And this whole queen-of-the-world routine just bugs me.

She makes no attempt to hide her anger and disgust. I arch an eyebrow. 'Oh, I get it. You don't make mistakes.'

'No, I don't.' She strides across to the sinks, twists the tap on and shoves her brushes underneath.

'Wow. Life must be easy if you're born perfect.'

'Born perfect?' she echoes coldly. She shakes the brushes dry, then gives a self-righteous shrug. 'At least I'm not ordinary.'

It's supposed to be an insult, of course. I still remember back in primary school when we had to look up the meaning of our name. I found out that Sarah meant princess and for weeks I carried around the guilt of thinking I had failed my parents. Princesses are beautiful and blonde. I was a feral eight-year-old with big feet, unmanageable hair and a habit of losing things. Not regal at all.

Yet if there's one thing I've learned it's that I don't want to be a princess anyway. Of course I want to do extraordinary things, but I don't ever want to get to the point where I look down my nose at people like she does, and think I'm better than them. And I don't want the attention on me.

I pass Morgan in the corridor on my way to last period. She grabs my arm. 'Hey, where were you on Friday? I wanted to show you one of my photos.'

'I took a day off. Where were you today?'

'Debating. Well, getting ready for a debate tomorrow. Bludging.' She grins.

'Does Sarah Bancroft hate everybody's guts or just mine?' I ask suddenly.

'Yeah, she's got issues.'

'Tell me about it.'

'Seriously, though…' Morgan leans in closer, confidential. 'Her mum hanged herself last year. Her dad was about to get remarried and everything, big drama. I heard Sarah was the one who actually found her. That's gotta screw someone up, right?'

There's something about the way she says it. Not exactly blasé but with a sort of morbid enthusiasm. It makes me feel a little sad. Not for myself, but for how naive I once was; for how naive you're able to be when nothing truly terrible has ever happened to you.

I picture Sarah Bancroft in my mind, that stiff arrogance. Makes a lot of sense, now. Must be hard to turn up every day knowing everybody knows your story.

*

Mum's car is in the garage, and based on the almost overpowering smell of roasted coffee, I guess she's been home for a while. I find her in the lounge room sitting on the couch. Iago is beside her, head on her lap. She never lets him on the couch…

'Mum?'

She and Iago both look up, and I see. She's crying. And when Mum cries, she cries. She's got mascara and tissues everywhere.

'Mum…'

'I'm all right.'

'Yeah, sure you are.'

I'm not panicking because it's obviously not anything too sudden or terrible. *Still*…the trouble feeling starts to burn in my stomach. Is this about Alan?

'What happened?'

'Nothing. Nothing happened…I just…' She's on the verge. Trembling. And there she goes…She starts to sob. 'I don't want Alan to go.'

'He doesn't have to go.'

'It's not that simple.'

Okay, I've never been in a relationship, so maybe I'm not the expert. But I don't understand how it can be so complicated. I know they love each other. 'Just talk to him, Mum. He still loves you. He just doesn't want you to shut him out all the time.'

She sniffs, blows her nose noisily.

'Go on that holiday with him.' I pass her the box of

tissues. 'You guys need to spend some time together.'

'What about you? We can't—' she sniffs. 'We can't just leave you.'

If that's her biggest argument I think I've pretty much won this one. I watch as she blows her nose, then tries to mop up her mascara.

She looks at me over the top of the tissue. 'You're settling in all right, aren't you?'

'At school? Yeah.'

'I wasn't sure whether a new school would be best for you...'

I've never had any doubt about that. Morgan's comments have only proved me right. I couldn't have handled going back to my old school, knowing that everybody knew what happened, seeing constant reminders. But it's more than just that; I'm not the same person I was a year ago. I'm new, too.

Anthony was right. Morgan is good, way better than the rest of the cast. The way she talks, moves across the stage, is assured and commanding, convincing. Kayla didn't say much in the car, but I'm glad to have her beside me, and at the end she's on her feet clapping for Morgan when she takes a bow. For the briefest second Morgan catches my eye, and there's a flicker of something—recognition? gratitude?—before she looks away again.

On the way home we talk about the play, about Morgan. I'm feeling restless after sitting still, and with frustration and uncertainty still jostling for prime position in my mind the last thing I want to do is go home and go to bed.

I climb out of the car and look across the roof at Kayla. 'I'm going to get changed and go for a run.'

'Want some company?'

I don't want to look too eager; I pretend to think about it. For maybe a second. 'Okay.'

We take a different route this time, a longer track through the valley. I've spent my whole life in this suburb, and covered most of it by foot dozens of times, but it's been years since I've gone this way. I let Kayla lead the way, trusting her, feeling safe in the silence as we run. I never realised how different it would feel to have company, to not feel like I'm the only one in the world.

We're heading down Third Street, about to pass the top of Roberts Road. I gesture to the right. 'This way.'

It's been demolished. The long driveway that led to the carpark in front of the indoor pools now leads to nowhere. Just piles of dirt and weeds, a desolate moonscape under the fluorescent street lights. The fence along one side of the outdoor pool still remains, absurdly, with those purple flowers I remember growing on vines entwined in the mesh like a trellis. I can't even tell where the big brick building housing the indoor pools used to be. Even the banana tree where Lauren and I waited for Mum is gone. It's as if the fragile foundations of my life are literally being bulldozed into nonexistence.

'What happened?'

Kayla kicks at a plastic marker flag in the ground.

'Looks like they're subdividing.'

Morgan, Mum, Lauren, even Dad…and for some reason it's seeing this site bulldozed that breaks me. I'm five again and my mum's late because my dad walked out on her, Lauren's mad and Morgan's crying and I'm too scared to say anything. Then and now. The tears that have been a dead weight in my chest for so long are threatening to bubble up.

I swallow hard. Not here. Not now. You don't cry like a baby in front of a girl, especially when you're still trying to work out if the girl in question even likes you. If I cry now, she'll never look at me again. I'll never be able to look at her.

'Want to cut through to—' Turning, she breaks off when she sees me. 'What?'

I can't answer her, I just shrug, stare up at the sky and try to think of anything other than the possibility of shameful tears. I can't do it anymore. I can't be the only one in the house who is trying to fix things. I can't even remember a time when I wasn't caught between Lauren and Mum and Morgan's tantrums. How is that fair? It can't just be me, I'm not strong enough. And if that's too much, how could I even think about having another girl's feelings to worry about?

I can actually feel the hot tears smarting in my eyes. I turn away quickly, before she can see them. The humiliation burns just as badly. I really am just the weakling Lauren says I am.

There's debris all over the ground and I reach down and grab the first thing I find. It's a broken piece of brick. I hurl it as far as I can into the empty lot, watching it bounce and tumble on the rough ground before rolling to a stop. It feels good to do something, so I grab another thing—a stick—and throw that too. A chunk of sandstone the size of a baseball follows that. I'm reaching for another stick when I see Kayla in my peripheral vision, grabbing a large piece of a branch—a few dried leaves still hanging on—and tossing it like a javelin. She lets out a whoop as she tosses a rock after it, exultant. I could be angry that she's hijacking my catharsis, but strangely, it lifts my spirits. I toss another piece of brick, watching it bounce off a piece of concrete slab downhill and roll out of sight. Beside me, Kayla scavenges piece after piece of debris, tossing them long, high, underarm like bowling balls or swung like a discus, whooping and laughing. Despite myself, I start to laugh too. Eventually we run out of things to throw. She spins a little on the spot, like a little girl making herself dizzy, and I'm half expecting her to fall dramatically to the ground when she suddenly grabs my shoulders and jumps up onto my back, wrapping her legs around my waist, piggyback. I nearly topple with the sudden impact and her weight, but I don't.

I manage to stay upright, reflexively wrapping my arms around her legs to hold her steady. She doesn't weigh as much as I expected, once I get my balance.

All that energy constantly radiating from her made her seem bigger.

Her laughter dies down but she's breathing heavily from her efforts. I feel—and hear—her breath at my ear, and then something soft—her lips?—on my cheek.

'You're crazy,' I manage.

'Yeah, but doesn't it feel good?'

It does. Oh, it does. If she'd tried to talk to me, if she'd been sympathetic, I think it would have just made things worse. But…

'You're going to make a good psychologist.'

'Thank you.' And with that, she frees herself from my grip and hops down, brushing herself off. 'C'mon, let's walk home.'

We don't say much on the way back. I'm a bit too overwhelmed to think what to say. All I know is that I want to be with her. Crazy and scary as she is, I think I'm in love.

I don't know if I'm supposed to kiss her goodbye, but she saves me having to make a move. She just smiles, a coy, teasing smile that is like a shot of vodka warming my insides, and disappears into her house.

Our house is dark, the only light coming from Lauren's room. She's standing by her bed with piles of clothes, toiletries and her forty-litre backpack spread out on her bed. Less than a month since she unpacked it, and she's taking off again already. I'm not surprised.

'Where are you going?'

She shrugs. 'Auckland, to start. After that, I don't know.'

'What about uni?'

Another shrug. She doesn't know. I watch her for a second, her hands as they methodically fold and pack. Still with that swift efficiency, but lacking the certainty, the confidence that have always defined her.

'I can't stay here.' Quietly.

I don't ask her why not. Maybe I already know. I feel it a bit, too. But her way of dealing is just to run away, and I can't believe there isn't a better way, something that makes it better for everybody, not just the one.

She stares morosely ahead. 'She's not wrong, you know. I mean, the writing thing, it's stupid. But pouring your life out for a cause…that's not wrong.'

Even if it makes you hate everyone and everything? I wonder. Even if it wrecks you for anything else?

'It has to be possible,' she says, as if she's read my thoughts. 'I just have to figure out how to do it. Sort myself out first, I guess. Find inner peace, all that crap. After all…life is short.'

I wonder about the guy she was with before, and try to picture someone brave enough to be with my sister. Did he have the same burning ambition to save the world? And, like her, did he just not know how to make it work?

'There's always therapy,' I quip.

'Yeah, right.' Her lip curls up in a smile, and I know she's thinking the same thing I am. None of us would ever dream of seeing a shrink. We just weren't raised that way. Mum would disown us.

Most of the time I feel like we're worlds apart, strangers in the same house. But at times like this the bond between us—at least, the shared memory of the crap we survived—feels firm, inviolable. My older sister is a judgmental control freak and an emotional screw-up whose biggest enemy is her own pig-headedness, but sometimes she can be…all right. I guess that's what gives me the courage to ask her.

'When's your flight?'

'Sunday morning.'

'Morgan's play is at seven tomorrow tonight.'

'I'm not going.'

After tonight, I feel different. I'm not just the quiet one hiding in my room with the book. I'm the one that Kayla likes. I'm the one that Kayla kissed. What have I got to lose? Why not be reckless, take her on?

'Why not? Why can't you do something nice for once?'

My voice is louder than normal, bolder. She looks taken aback by it, but doesn't answer. Somehow that's all I need. 'What did we ever do to you? Why do you act like something terrible happened that you have to keep running away from? It's like you hate us and Mum and this house so much that you can't stand to be around us.

224

What did we do to you that was so bad?'

She stands still, hands hanging by her side, just taking it. Her eyes are on the ground, face turned away as if to deflect the words, not have to meet my accusing gaze.

Slowly, she slides her hands into her front jeans pockets, digging them in deep. Looks up, but can't bring herself to look at me. Her gaze goes over my left shoulder.

'I got tired of nobody caring.'

I can tell she's trying hard to keep her voice steady, but I can still hear the tremor in it. I don't understand. What happened to her happened to all three of us. We were all rejected by Dad, then rejected by Mum. Now it's a struggle to get even Morgan to acknowledge I exist.

'I was here too,' I say, even though I know it won't be any consolation to her. 'They didn't care about me, either.'

She snorts. 'Are you kidding?' Rolls her eyes, as if she can't believe I could be so unaware. 'You could have asked her'—she points at the ceiling—'for *anything*. Anything at all. She would have given it to you. Not that you even cared. You always had your own little world where everything had a happy ending.'

Her tone is contemptuously offhand, coloured by the same bitterness that was in Morgan's voice. I stare at her, feeling stupid for not recognising it sooner. Replaying, in my mind, Mum wandering down to talk to me as I sat on the back step, loading me up with books... Even more reason for Lauren to despise me, for Morgan to feel as though we weren't on equal footing. But grossly unfair if they thought that was ever something I wanted.

I fumble for words. 'I never asked for any of that. And I never ignored you. You're the one who ignored us and just...left.'

It doesn't seem like an argument either one of us is going to win. I draw a breath and try to get back to my original point. 'Dad left all three of us. Mum ignored all three of us. Can we at least try to be decent to each other, and go to Morgan's play?'

She looks over at the piles of clothes neatly stacked on the bed. She's probably thinking about wherever it is she'll end up, where there's no parents or siblings or anybody else who's supposed to care. Exhales. 'Fine.'

She takes a step back towards the bed, as if the conversation's over, but I'm not done. I've spent my life being affected by Lauren's experiences, moods and words. Isn't it about time I had my own impact?

'I think Mum should come along. I tried to get her to come last night, she wasn't interested. Can you try?'

She turns back, visibly impatient with me now. I'm pushing it. 'Why does it matter so much?'

'Because it matters to Morgan.'

She glances past me, one way then the other, as if

226

looking for somebody to help her out. Finally sighs. 'Okay. I'll take care of it.'

And there it is again, just like when we were kids. I believe her.

We almost make it out of Singleton before Izzy changes lanes and suddenly swings off the main road, throwing up gravel with her back tyres. Tash, already crying in the back, gets louder.

'Can you give her the Panadol and shut her up?'

Tash is terrible at taking medicine at the best of times. Right now, she's confused and upset as well as sick. Kicks me away. Knocks the measuring cup in my hand. Spills all over her and splatters Izzy's back seat. Stupid kid.

'Stop it! I'm trying to make you feel better.'

Pour another capful. Sloshes as I pour. She kicks at me again, tears and snot streaming down her face. Starts to howl. I lose it.

'You don't want my help? Fine!' Stupid kid. I'm

over it. She's had enough chances. Time to undo this mistake. Time to get free.

Yank her out of the car seat. She's scared of the dark, but so what? She's already crying anyway. Pry her stupid sticky fingers off me and dump her on the ground, in the gravel. Slam the door shut. 'You can stay here.'

Climb back into the passenger seat and slam it closed after me. Grab my seatbelt and push it into the slot. Still fuming, mad, sick of her, sick of who I've ended up being, sick of everything. Kick at the dashboard in front of me. Turn to Izzy. 'What are you waiting for?'

Her mouth is half-open. Stunned. More than that, shit-scared. Sits for a moment, disbelieving. A funny choked sound comes out of her throat. She pushes her door open and just about falls out of the car, running around the bonnet to the other side, where Tash is.

I still feel numb. Part of me knows how irrational, how irresponsible, how unbelievably terrible my action was. The rest of me is just too tired to care. Who have I been trying to kid? I'm not up to this. Why should I be? I'm seventeen. I'm not supposed to be a parent. I'm still a kid myself.

Izzy—Izzy who is grossed out by runny noses and sticky fingers—stands outside the car with Tash, still screaming away, in her arms. Maybe trying to soothe her, just as likely trying to figure out what to do. I draw my knees up and rest my head between them, arms wrapped over the top, and all I can think of is my bedroom in

Terry and Rose-Marie's house. My bed, my pillows, my doona and blanket. Like a little kid, I suddenly want nothing more.

Hear the back door open. Tash still crying. Izzy strapping her in. Keep my head down, keep myself buried. I know she's going to ask, to want to know. I don't know how I can tell her.

My holy grail, my carefully nurtured secret. This is airhead Izzy. How could she possibly understand how desperately I need to see, to know? She can't comprehend how unfair it is that no matter how much I read and try to remember and try to do the right thing, I'll never reach that deep recess of my mind where I've stored my mother's face. I'll never know my real name. If I ever even had one.

The back door closes again, quietly. Hear her climb into the driver's seat. Doesn't ask anything. Doesn't say anything. Just starts up the car and puts the radio on, tuning into a local station.

I think back to my list, to those last four names. Izzy who doesn't have any more of a clue about life than I do. Easy enough to blame her for all the partying; except I'm the one who got stoned every weekend at twelve and knocked up at fourteen. Probably learned half of what she knows from me.

Terry who really did make me smile. Made me feel like I could be the better person he wanted me to be. Rose-Marie who honestly did think she was rescuing me. Not her fault I kept jumping back into the water. And Tash…

'Can you take us home, please?' My voice is small and muffled through my arms and legs.

'That's what I'm doing.' Sounds serious, and mad, too. Doesn't look in my direction at all. Maybe she's realising what she should have known all along, that she'd be better off without me. My whole life all I've ever done is screw things up, then take off somewhere else and do it all over again.

Completely dark by the time we reach the freeway. Stare out the window, brain still too heavy to think properly. Tash nods off in the back seat. Izzy fiddles with the radio station and her CDs, but doesn't speak. Guess she doesn't know what to say. Watch the lights of the cars coming towards us, wondering what sort of people are in them, what sort of lives they lead. Close my eyes and think about the day Tash was born, when I told myself I had to do this right, I couldn't let this be just another thing I stuffed up.

We reach the end of the freeway and Izzy pulls into a petrol station. 'We're just about empty.'

She climbs out to fill up. I unlatch my seatbelt and look back to Tash for the first time since I dumped her by the side of the road. Her face is flushed, dried snot hanging from her nose. Try to remember if the Panadol is somewhere in the back seat or if I threw it out of the car before. Don't know. Put my hand on her forehead.

She jerks awake. My hand is cold, and her face is still hot and sweaty. Must be dehydrated, too. Hasn't had anything to drink since she threw her Tippee cup at me. She's awake but groggy.

Izzy opens my car door and hands me her wallet. 'You go pay. You know my PIN. Get some water, too.'

Obviously doesn't trust me alone with Tash. I don't blame her. Some small part of me is actually impressed. Pity it's taken something like this to get some maturity out of her.

I find the Panadol bottle, with lid tightly fixed, on the floor of the back seat. Offer it to Izzy. She shakes her head. 'Do it when you get back.'

I get the medicine into her this time, then offer her the refilled Tippee cup and a handful of jellybeans. She sucks at the water for a while but doesn't eat the jellybeans. Just holds them tightly in one hand, her cup in the other. Feel like I should apologise, but I know it's not words that people remember, it's actions. Bit late to undo mine.

They tried and failed to find my parents. Department of Child Services tried, reporters tried, some of my foster parents tried. Nobody ever found anything. I didn't match any records of missing children. Nobody called up to claim me. Nobody ever wanted me.

The sky is dark with storm clouds when I get home.

Seems fitting, symbolic of the shitstorm that is my life, gathering to unleash its grand finale. Front door opens before I can fit my key in the lock. Both Rose-Marie and Terry are there, still in work clothes. Tash is heavy in my arms, not asleep but not fully awake, either. The Panadol should have kicked in by now but she still feels hot.

'Where—' Rose-Marie starts the question but then cuts herself off. 'Is that a rash?'

Start to cry. Not out of guilt, though I feel that, or out of exhaustion, though I feel that too. But because even though I hate her taking control and telling me what to do, she's the closest thing to a mother I've got, and despite all the crap I've given her, she actually does care. And Terry, who looks like he wants for all the world to be mad at me, and rightfully so...Takes Tash from my arms and passes her to Rose-Marie, then he opens his arms and draws me against him. I can feel his chest quickly expand and tighten as if he's finding it hard to get a proper breath. Speaks, his breath blowing my hair. 'We thought you weren't coming back.'

Rose-Marie sits Tash on the kitchen counter, under the fluorescent lights. Starts to check her, lifting the long-sleeved t-shirt to see her stomach, her back; peeling back the sleeves to see her arms. Red rash, everywhere. Terry gets a cold washer and the thermometer. I hang back, standing against the fridge, while they discuss the rash: the chances of it being meningococcal, or a symptom of some virus or simply an allergic reaction to the medication the doctor prescribed. They're quiet and calm, weighing the pros and cons like seasoned professionals. Which they are. Which I'm not.

Terry decides they should take her to the hospital, just in case.

'Do you want to come or stay here?'

'I'll stay.' My voice, like my chest, is tight. I watch them go, Tash's head lolling on Terry's shoulder. Maybe it's their calmness. I don't feel worried about her. She's in safe hands. They'll know what to do, what decisions to make, how to take care of her. All those things I can't do.

The house is still and quiet. Nearly ten. I turn slowly. Take it all in, memorise it all. Tash's drawings on the fridge. The fruit bowl I gave Rose-Marie last birthday and she's diligently displayed ever since. Typical household hums and tickings and cooking smells. Maybe if I hadn't been so busy fighting it I would have known this was home.

My bedroom, with bed still unmade after my too-few hours' sleep. Laptop sitting placidly, power light blinking. Clothes and pyjamas strewn around the place. My picture stuck to the ceiling above my head. Piles of books and magazines. Stuff piled up on my shelves, filling my wardrobe. So much stuff. Who was I kidding? I had it good here. They probably spent twice as much on me over the years as they have on Tash. My own TV, DVD player, fridge, laptop, all the clothes I could ever need…They deserved more in return.

My big travel bag is still half packed from before. Tip the contents out onto the floor. Start carefully repacking, taking only as much as I need. A few pairs of jeans, tops and a jacket, my uniform for tomorrow, shoes.

Never cried before about leaving a house. Pull my bedroom door closed. Start to cry. Can't stop.

I show Morgan my photos. I spread them out on the spare desk in the darkroom. I'll have to show Shepherd eventually but for now I only want Morgan to see. As it is I'm nervous as I watch her sift through them.

The photos of me and my scar, and a stack of over a hundred video stills, printed out at Target. Me tearing down my photo wall, and then six of Robbie, the camera right in his face, him giving it the thumbs-up. Last, but not least, another dozen digital prints, these ones different from the rest. Taken with the digital SLR I borrowed from school last year to take photos for my major work, ironically enough, but I got distracted by a thunderstorm, by the lightning bolts shooting through the sky.

Morgan examines everything thoroughly, taking it all in. 'DSLR?' she asks finally, pointing to the lightning photos.

'Canon 600D, 35mm prime lens.'

'Nice.'

She's sifted them into the different piles: Robbie photos; lightning, scar, wall. Whether she's worked the order out or is just guessing I don't know. I haven't told her about Robbie; it's just been easier not to. Today is the third of May. Exactly one week from today it will be a year since it happened. Mum and Alan are going to be in France. I don't know if Alan planned that on purpose, or if that's just the way it worked out, but I think it's a good idea. Mum's trying to cope better, but I don't think she's ready for the anniversary of his death.

Morgan points to the photos of Robbie. 'Your brother?'

'Yeah.'

'He looks like you.'

'He's dead.'

She takes the news quietly, as if she somehow already knew. Thinks it through. 'In that car crash? When your leg was hurt?'

'Yeah.'

I pick up one of the stills from the video of me tearing down my photo wall. Nearly two hundred photos plastered on that one wall. Two hundred moments in my life caught forever, or at least till I threw them out. Two hundred times my family or friends rolled their eyes and commented that I couldn't be taken anywhere without taking photos, and holding everyone else up in the process. Our undoing, in the end.

'You want to hear how it happened?' I ask suddenly, feeling courageous.

Morgan half shrugs, half nods, serious. 'Only if you want.'

It's something I went over again and again while I was in the hospital, five months for it to go round and round my head as I endured surgeries and setbacks and antibiotics for infections and physical rehab. I could have re-enacted it second by second. I recite it slowly, carefully, not so much reliving it but thinking as I speak that this is the first time in nearly a year that I've told this story.

It was the night of that huge storm. I was outside, taking photos of the lightning.

My phone, in my pocket, buzzes again. I know it's Robbie, calling to remind me I have to pick him up. His English class saw a play tonight at the Seymour Centre at Sydney Uni. I should have left already, but…I just need one more.

It's a deluge. It bounces off every surface, dances, splashes, fills the air. My hair is sticking to my scalp, matted on my face. I don't think there's a dry inch of me. One more photo, then a towel, then Robbie.

The camera is barely recognisable, swaddled in plastic bags and Gladwrap, bound with brown packaging tape. A plastic burka. The wind catches under an untaped edge of plastic around the lens and it starts to flap, but the noise is lost in the constant patter of driving rain and the roar of the wind.

There. And I've missed it. A crack of lightning ahead, to the right, in what would have been a perfectly framed shot between the two dead gum trees. The roll of thunder follows only a fraction of a second later.

The house phone inside is ringing. Tough luck, buddy. Mum and Alan are out, you'll just have to wait for me. One more shot. My other hand is reaching for the shutter release, praying for one more strike.

I steady the tripod as a particularly strong gust of wind shakes it, and, when it passes, find the dangling cable. There's splashes on the lens. Impossible to keep it dry, to find anything left to dry it with. I press it with my thumb, feeling it lock in. One thousand, two thousand...

As if on cue, a crack and the sky lights up. Impeccable timing. Thunder on its heels—the storm is getting closer.

Four thousand, five thousand, six thousand...Another whipcrack, somewhere behind me, and then something whizzes right past, hits the metal drainpipe behind me with a zing. A barrage of sharp pings on the roof, above the sound of the rain and the wind. Hailstorm.

Ten thousand, eleven thousand...I reach for the cable,

release it, hear or at least imagine the shutter snap closed. Through the murky plastic the image appears. Purple sky, spidery white bolts, green light along the horizon. Eerie. Beautiful. Perfect.

The driving wind rocks the tripod, legs start to bow. Hail now pelting down, flying in at all angles. A piece grazes my knuckles, ice burn. Heavenly shrapnel.

The camera. Knuckles will heal for free, but lenses are expensive and LCD screens easily damaged. I grab the tripod by its neck, draw the camera against me, smothered against wet clothes.

Inside, ignoring the puddle forming at my feet, I free the camera from the tripod and try to brush the water off the plastic coverings, cautious of getting the camera itself wet. I want to see the photo properly, check it's as good as it looked on the review screen.

My phone rings again, Robbie. I pick it up, and his voice fills my ears, stressed. It's getting pretty late. 'Are you coming or what?'

'Yeah, I'm on my way. Right now. Promise. I'll be there in under half an hour.'

I hang up, peeling my wet clothes off as I go. If Robbie's mad at me I'll tell him he's lucky to get picked up at all, he should be thankful to have a big sister willing to drive all that way on a rainy night to get him.

That's all it was. Me wanting that last shot, making me late to pick him up, so we were sitting there at that intersection at that wrong moment...Twenty minutes earlier the *street lights and the traffic lights had been working. Robbie and I would have got home in one piece. I'd be at uni right now studying photography and Robbie would be sitting at home playing his Xbox and life would be easy again, just like it always was.*

'What about if you included some of your other photos, too?' Morgan asks slowly.

'What other photos?'

'The ones you've been doing in here. The architecture ones. They'd fit, wouldn't they? Show the contrast? Your concept…'

That buildings outlast us. Robbie used to always think about that. He's the one I stole the concept from. We'd be driving down a street full of old houses and he'd start thinking aloud about the fact that the people who built the houses, who lived their lives out in them, were gone and for the most part forgotten. Going to Europe and walking through the millennia-old streets blew his mind.

'Think about how many millions of people have climbed these steps. Think about it. In a hundred years, is there going to be any evidence that we existed? You and me, I mean, and Mum and Alan. Maybe we'll have grandkids who'll still be alive and remember that we once existed, but nobody who really knew us. And in another hundred years after that, or two or three hundred years after that…Do you think there'll be any trace of our street? Our house will be flattened and they'll build highrises on top and there'll never be any trace that we were even alive…'

I loved that he thought about that sort of thing. I used to tell him to shut up and stop being so pretentious, trying to be all philosophical, but secretly I was glad he wasn't dumb like all the other boys, only interested in girls and sport.

'Maybe one day they'll make a statue of you,' I told him once. I was only teasing and he knew it, but he loved the idea.

I think of my artwork and I think of Robbie. It's not a statue, but it's the closest you'll get from me, brother of mine, at least for now.

After school, Iago and I go bush. It's almost four but the sky is still clear and blue and the leaves are floating leisurely on their branches. I always feel safe in the bush, insulated against whatever else is going on in my world. But more than that, I feel okay again. I can draw in a deep breath and release it and all I'm thinking about is how green the leaves are and the feel of the slight breeze on my bare arms.

Iago has run ahead. I find him waiting patiently for me, tail wagging. 'Yeah, yeah.'

He grins at me and takes off down the slope to the creek. I follow him down, careful as always because there's a lot of loose dirt and if I slip I'll end up in the water.

I stretch out on my tree, and I think, oddly enough, about Sarah Bancroft. Wondering if she hates me because she looks at me and thinks I'm somebody who has never known pain. Or maybe because she sees it in me, somehow, and that just makes her hate me all the more.

I think over Alan's words, that we can't always control what happens to us, we can only control what we do about it. He's right. Maybe that's how he can be so steady when it seems like the rest of the world is caving in. He's not trying to find someone to blame or some simple answer to it all. Because it's not simple. Every one of us—who and what we are—is the product of other people's choices as well as our own. With billions of people on the planet all living their ordinary lives, how could we possibly track the cause and effect of any one, single event? Robbie and I were in the car at that intersection at that moment because I was running late. But if he hadn't been at the play on that particular night, or there hadn't been a thunderstorm, or Mum and Alan hadn't been out at a dinner party, or any one of a thousand other scenarios, things would have worked out differently. We can't change what happened. The other driver probably wishes she could, but she can't either. All we can do is live knowing that we're part of the bigger picture, and that stuff happens but we can't let it ruin us.

*

Above me is a leaf dangling by a single spiderweb thread. It twists one way, then spins back the other, endlessly dancing without a breath of wind. I listen to Iago snuffling in the undergrowth and I watch my leaf and I know it's okay, I'm okay, whatever happens now.

It's the thud that wakes me, a crash outside my bedroom window. I jump out of bed and pull the curtains apart just in time to watch a pile of bound manuscripts fall from above. In the old trackies I wear as pyjamas, I head to Mum's room and find her at the window with a box full of books, extra copies of one of her earlier novels. 'What are you doing?'

'Did I do it wrong?'

'Do what wrong?'

'Everything. Have I been a bad mother?'

I don't answer her. I can't. She goes on. 'My own mother was always interfering in my life. I was so determined to let you make your own choices, your own mistakes. I thought I was doing the right thing.'

'Mum…' My stomach is starting to wrap itself up at her words. Did Lauren speak to her? What did she say? 'Can you put the box down? If that lands on somebody you could kill them.'

I watch her lower it to the ground. Try to summon some calm, or at least the appearance of calm.

'There's still one more night of the play. You haven't missed it. They've got the closing night tonight.'

'She doesn't even want me there.'

It doesn't take a genius to call Morgan's bluff. I feel frustration rising up in me at Mum using it as an excuse. 'So? Go anyway.'

She looks down at the box at her feet as if it will give her answers. Finally she shrugs. 'All right.'

Morgan doesn't emerge from her bedroom till almost midday, wandering into the kitchen in her baggy pyjamas to pour herself Coco Pops. I'm sitting at the counter with the newspaper spread out in front of me, but I'm not reading it.

'You doing anything today?'

Spoonful of cereal in hand, she looks up at me, suspicion crossing her face, like I'm about to ask her to help me with something unpleasant. 'Why?'

'I just thought we could hang out or something.'

That same suspicion, like she sees right through me, and hates me for trying to bridge the gap. She shakes her head. 'I just want to stay home.'

'I've been thinking about going to see Dad. Or calling him up, maybe. I don't know.'

'Why?'

I'm not sure I even know the answer to that myself. Am I really ready to have him as part of my life? Would he even want to be? Or is it just closure he's after, forgiveness? What would it mean for us?

It's hard to explain the feeling that's starting to burn inside me, of seeing the possibilities, realising how much I actually want out of this life. I've never cared, before. I've never thought enough to myself to know I deserved better. 'Because we need to make our world bigger, not smaller.'

We settle for an email. Cowardly, maybe, but it's a start. Morgan sits cross-legged on her bed as I type it, chewing on her thumbnails the whole time, offering suggestions as we go. We tell him about what subjects we're doing at school, about Lauren's travels, Morgan's play. Lame stuff, but safe ground to start on.

The mouse hovers over the send button. I look over to her. 'Send it?'

A long moment. She nods. 'Yeah.'

I don't know how it makes her feel but my heart is pounding as I click the send button. Not entirely panic, though. There's exhilaration in it, too, like I've thrown the dice and I don't know what's going to happen but I don't really have anything to lose.

For a long minute we stare at the email screen, as if expecting a reply to arrive. Finally I shut the lid and Morgan looks at me. 'Thanks. You're a pretty good brother sometimes.'

That's about as good as it'll ever get from Morgan, I know. At least she's willing to say it. I think Lauren would rather sew her mouth shut.

The doorbell rings. By the time I get there Lauren has already opened it. Kayla stands on the doorstep, in her leggings and a t-shirt, ready for a run.

I stop in the hallway, feeling the ghost of warmth from her touch, the way she clung on my back and whispered in my ear. Lauren gives me a look, eyebrow raised. Then she makes a 'do what you want, you're the one who has to live with it' shrug, and she strides past me and disappears into her room.

Kayla watches her go. Her eyes are sparkling and her lips curve in an amused smile at my sister. I have never, in my life, felt more compelled to kiss someone. It's like a physical force trying to pull me towards her.

I step closer, and as I do I see past her, to something on the lower step. 'What—?'

She steps to the side and gestures to it, like a TV hostess displaying a prize. 'I made you shelves.'

I can't think of a time ever in my life anybody has made anything for me. Mum was never the sort to knit or sew stuff. She never saw the point. I never even had grandparents or aunts who made toys or clothes. The last handmade gift I got was probably a card about ten years ago, and even that was more my sisters being cheap than actually caring enough to craft something for me.

'You made shelves,' I repeat, staring. They're about waist high, a metre squared with three shelves, stained a dark brown. They look like shelves you would buy in a furniture shop, nothing like the pile of plywood I saw in her garage.

'You have books piled up all over your room. I figured you could use some shelves.'

She's right. I've never had enough shelf space for all my books. They live stacked up on my desk, on the floor, in the top of my wardrobe. But Kayla has never been in my bedroom, or at least not since we were about six…

'How did you—?'

'I can see into your room from mine. I made them to match the rest of your furniture. Walnut stain.' She pauses, grinning at me. 'Is that too psycho-stalker next door?'

It probably is, but somehow I don't care. She made me shelves. She really likes me.

'I like you,' I blurt out, because it's that or I do jump on her and kiss her.

Her eyes sparkle all the more. 'Good.'

The house is quiet when I get back from our jog. I have a quick shower, and then I go upstairs to Mum.

She's not asleep this time. She's standing in front of

her full-length mirror, wearing dark jeans and a green knitted jumper, the colour she always used to wear because it brought out her eyes and showed off the copper of her hair. A silk scarf, because she thinks it looks arty, and her tweed coat on the bed, ready to go. I watch as she holds up one set of earrings, then another, trying to decide.

She chooses one pair and stands straighter, studying her reflection. How long since she's dressed up? She hasn't been to signings or readings in years, and she has most of her meetings with her editors here or over the phone.

Lauren is waiting for us downstairs, holding her jacket impatiently. She was already set to go before, when I returned from my run with Kayla, still grinning despite myself.

'Are we going or what?'

I must have been only nine or ten when I first dreamed the dream. Every time I dream it, it's as though I'm right back there, a skinny, shy fourth-grader.

By that point Mum's writing had become a firmly entrenched part of our family life. In my dream she came home one day with a shiny clunky metal thing.

'A shredder,' she says. 'For turning paper into snow.' Then she starts to pull all her old bundles of manuscripts down from the top of the wardrobe, where Dad once kept his things, ripping the brown paper off one and feeding

the cover sheet through. We watch with goosebumps as the machine churns and the paper is sliced into long, white strips.

'I want to try! My turn!' we all cry, and Mum stands aside to let us slice open the bundles and feed the pages through, never once pausing to look at the closely typed words covering them. Morgan is sent running to fetch buckets to catch the strips, and when we finish the last pages Mum stands at the top of the stairs and tips the bucketfuls down over us, one at a time, letting the pieces float down like snow, while we dance underneath like the heathens our grandmother says we are.

Among my sisters' squeals I found myself falling silent as I stood, watching the paper snow falling, falling, and I felt something spreading through me, a slow rush of relief like a breeze through my veins. Time stopped, and I floated, and my body was separate from my mind and my thoughts. I looked up, and my mother was standing at the top of the stairs, last bucket emptied, leaning against the railing and staring as I was at the floating pieces, seeing them like I was, slowly, slowly, like falling snow. And in my dream, even at eight, I could feel, if not understand, what a powerful moment it was. Only years later did I discover the word for it. Catharsis.

The show is sold out, so we stand up the back, watching not just the action on the stage but the reaction from the audience. There's an energy to the show tonight, more confidence than last time, and it shows.

I stand between them, Mum on my right and Lauren on my left, watching, feeling their warmth and hearing their breathing. Conscious that this might be the last time we'll be together for a long time to come. Feeling some sort of peace between us, something of that moment in the dream where everything slowed down and it brought us all together, flawed as we are.

My sister will go to New Zealand, and maybe she will sort herself out, and find inner peace and all that crap. Mum will keep writing, because she doesn't know what else to do, but maybe she'll find a way of balancing that with caring about our lives. Maybe I'll get better at reminding her to do it.

Falling, falling like snow. Clapping.

Knowing that this one act, this one moment, isn't everything; but hoping it will be enough.

Paper snow and peace rushing like wind through my veins. Catharsis.

before
after
later

Wipe my tears and runny nose on the back of my sleeve. Try not to think of her. Try to think of anything, anything at all that will hurt less, like the stupid things I've done and the poor abused kids whose lives mine has collided with, but those things, those stupid things that have kept me awake so many nights, are completely outweighed by the single thought, the single word. One stupid little accident who means more to me than anyone and anything else ever could.

I'm proving myself, Terry. Proving I do know the best thing for Tash, and that it's not me. Won't be long till she's making permanent memories and it's the best thing for her if I'm not in them. Might just be the only decent thing I'll ever do for her.

*

Rain. Starts with just a splatter or two, then starts pelting down, makes it hard to see. Makes me cry all the harder. God, if he's up there, is crying with me.

Rain gets heavier, starts pounding down. Terry's long-awaited low-pressure system in all its glory. Thunder and lightning start to roll and crack. Tash will be scared, she hates storms.

Street lights up ahead stutter and go off. Road is dark, with passing blurs of red tail-lights and flashes of headlights. Wind drives the rain under the eaves of the bus shelter. Shoes getting wet, jeans start to stick to my legs.

And then it all happens fast. Fast, but slow. A car, almost invisible in the dark and rain, no headlights, coming from my right. Black car. In front of me, head-lights surging suddenly out from the side street, white beams penetrating the haze of raindrops.

In my mind, somehow calm, aware of the inevitability: they're going to hit. There's about to be a collision.

Half step backwards, as if the bus shelter will protect me.

Neither car has time to stop, and the brakes screech and wheels lock and start to swerve but not enough and they're going to hit.

I physically recoil at the moment of impact. Trip on my bag, put a hand out to catch myself, unable to draw my eyes away. Cars crumpling into each other. Flinch away, eyes squeezed shut. Hearing the tear and crunch of metal long after it's actually stopped; feeling it like a slow-motion slamming punch to the face.

Open. Watch. Both cars spinning, spinning, and then slowing, like the end of a teacup ride at Disneyland. Don't know how long it actually takes. Feels like forever. Then a long second of deafening stillness.

I'm pretty sure someone just died.

Run. Door of the black car opens and a guy half falls out and starts puking on the road. Past him, to the white car, crumpled against the brick wall. Smoke pouring from the front half. Most of the bonnet gone, compacted into nothing. Front windscreen shattered.

Reach for the front passenger door. Doorframe is buckled, door jammed. Round to the other side, and the driver's door comes free. In the dark, make out a girl sitting there. My age, maybe. Not moving. Dead? Front of the car has caved in on her, airbag deflated.

In the passenger seat a boy, pinned by the bent frame of the car, chest swallowed up by the dislodged dashboard. Everything's covered in blood. Air smells like iron and gunpowder. Rain slices through the open door.

A sound, like a gurgle, from the girl. Sound of running footsteps coming up behind me. Step back into the full force of the pounding rain. Wet fringe sticking to me, getting in my eyes.

'Here,' I call. Shaky voice. 'I think she's still alive.'

She's alive. But he's dead.

Bile in my throat. Swallow it down.

The man's out of breath from running. Pushes past me, leans into the car, says something. Draws back, blood already on his shirtsleeves. Reaches into his pocket, then tosses me something. His phone, now with bloody fingerprints on it.

'Call an ambulance.'

Watch him with the girl in the car as I give the details to the operator. He gestures for the phone, and I hand it to him. Without asking, he grabs my hand and presses it down on the girl's thigh, his hand on top of mine, pushing so hard it hurts. Talks fast, out of breath. 'Keep pressure on this. Whatever you do, don't let go.'

Want to whimper or back off or say no but know that I can't. Lean over the girl, putting all my body weight on her leg. Feel the blood squirm between my fingers, warm and sticky. He touches my back. 'I'll be right back. Keep the pressure on.'

Listen to his shoes slapping the wet road as he runs. Count the long seconds. Watch the girl draw one shallow breath, then another. She moves slightly. Groans. After twenty-six seconds the footsteps return and a blinding light floods the car's interior.

'She still breathing?'

Squint, trying to see again. My eyes adjust and I see he's holding a heavy-duty torch in one hand and bag in the other. First-aid kit. Look back and see how very bright red the blood is, and try not to feel sick.

'I think she's waking up.'

He checks her again in the light. Points me to a black bag he's tossed on the ground. 'Find me a bandage, the big triangular one. And the shock blanket.'

He works. I follow instructions: find, hold, put pressure here. The girl stirs, groans as he wraps the bandage tightly around her thigh to keep the pressure on. People come, murmuring and trying to hold up umbrellas against the relentless rain. Sirens. Ambos push through and I step back, still holding spare wads of gauze in my bloodied hands. A police officer gently takes the gauze from me, and asks for my statement. I hear the girl crying in the car, horrible groaning sobs.

He stays with her, talking to her, helping the paramedics. Dozens of people here now—police and fire brigade and ambulance officers, all dressed in their reflective night gear, yelling terse instructions to each other in the rain and pushing the crowd back as it inches closer again and again. Give my statement, then sit on the bench in the bus shelter, watching as they start to cut the frame of the car away.

Think of Tash, head lolling on Terry's shoulder. Rose-Marie worrying about the rash. Know that some day I'll have what it takes to do the parenting thing right, but for now I need parents as much as Tash does. And all I want to do is go home.

*

Kitchen light's still on, weirdly normal. After the harsh light and shadows of the crash scene, it feels clean and safe and warm, even with nobody else home. Tash's newest drawing on the fridge. She's got the T and the S happening now.

Clothes are covered in blood, still wet after the rain. Peel them off and climb under the hot shower, watch the muddy brown water sluice down the drain. Put bloody clothes into the washing machine, unpack my bag, sit and wait.

Past one when they get home. Tash is asleep in Terry's arms. Never been so glad to see them, but I don't let on. Don't want to scare them.

'What did they say?'

'They think it's a reaction to the medicine. They've switched her onto a different one.'

Nod. Watch as he hands Tash to Rose-Marie. Tash stirs sleepily, thumb finding its way into her mouth. Rose-Marie carries her out of the room, off to bed.

Terry fetches himself a glass of water, then puts it down and looks at me. 'Are you okay?'

'Yeah.' Pause, wanting to say something, not wanting to sound mushy. Think of the family who'll be spending tonight in the hospital and won't go home with such a simple diagnosis. 'Just glad you guys are back.'

I gesture at the kitchen window. The rain is still hammering down outside, sheets of it sloshing against the glass. I hear a crack of lightning in the distance followed by a roll of thunder. 'Your rain finally arrived.'

He nods. 'The roads are chaos, took us an hour to get home.' He gestures to the window. 'This keeps up, we'll easily get a hundred and fifty, two hundred millimetres in the next thirty-six to forty-eight hours.'

He sounds like the weather forecaster he is, like he should have a map and a pointer. I don't care, though. Maybe on some subconscious level I'm remembering my various lives in the country, and how desperately everyone waited for rain. Or maybe it's the cathartic quality of it, torrents of water to wash me clean. Either way, I just find myself feeling ridiculously, soberly thankful for it.

In bed, staring up at my ceiling as I listen to the storm outside. Tracing the different sections with my eyes, rolling their names over my tongue, comforted by the routine. Look for a place to store today's experiences: long walk to school and the taste of not-enough-sleep. Exam hall. Car trip to Singleton with Tash whining in the back. That moment in Coles where I nearly had it. The crash, and the life I helped save. The death. The rain, flooding my parched soul.

I was wrong. How could I think abandoning Tash could be the best thing for her, when it's the thing that screwed up my life the most? Nobody wanted the little girl abandoned in the freezer aisle. But that's not me anymore, and it's not Tash. Rose-Marie might be an annoying tight-arse sometimes but she meant what she said. We're both wanted.

Reach for my bedside table, pulling the drawer open and digging through until I find the list from Mrs Perkins. Run my finger down the list of options. Psychiatry? Psychology? Neuroscience? Terry and Rose-Marie want me to go to uni. If I get my act together I can still get the marks for it.

Doctor Eliat Singleton.

Well, maybe.

acknowledgments

Many thanks to the team at Text Publishing and particularly my editor, the brilliant Mandy Brett, who knew exactly what I wanted to say, and how to say it better. Thanks to Irina Dunn for early manuscript advice and suggesting I submit to the Text Prize.

Thank you to my family for your support. To those of you who read early drafts: thank you for reading, and more importantly, for not laughing at my efforts!